KIMA BLAZE

The Curse of Sight

A RIFT IN THE VEIL: book 2

Contents

Introduction

The Spirit World has been dormant for years. Its denizens have slumbered, buried in their caves and roots and lakes. They have left the World Of Man alone for generations, sated and hibernating.

They would have stayed that way for generations more, if not for the rift.

One night, the Spirit World shook.

Its ground burst and steam hissed from the earth's heart. It dried out the lakes and burned the roots and collapsed the caves. It woke the denizens of the Spirit World, and they woke with a vengeance.

Angry to have their slumber interrupted. Hungry after decades of starvation.

Some of these were good spirits and soon turned to right the wrong of their world.

Others didn't care, and soon found new places to hibernate.

Others still wanted to sate their hunger, but there was no food for them in this world, and the gateways to the World Of Man had long since been closed.

They would have stayed in the Spirit World, starving now as the earth had burned everything except them, but the scent of live flesh and young spirits came to them on a wind of change.

But some of the hungry ones didn't have the energy to search out the source of the scent, and so forced their way back into hibernation.

Others died on their way to it.

Others tried making their own way.

Others found a new way.

These others found a rift in the fabric that made up the Spirit World. Fog poured through it, enveloping them. If they entered, they would walk through it, blind to each other. If they emerged, they would have passed through the moat between worlds.

They would step into the World Of Man.

1

So hungry. So weak. Need food. Need souls. Hungry... Eleanor was sitting in a rocking chair, dressed in bright yellow folds, and she stroked her big stomach, humming to it and every now and again murmuring words in French... Wait for dark. Time to hunt. Time to devour. Could smell them. A group of souls, just waiting to be food. So hungry... Sanderson was standing before a closed casket, which she knew was empty. She was dressed in black, her belly barely showing. Her face was dry, angry, as she cursed the men that stopped looking for her Martin. That doomed him to death. Her hand moved instinctually toward her stomach, but she stopped it. She couldn't handle the life in there. Not yet... Not far now. More running, and no more hungry. No more souls... Hungryyyyyy...

"...zzie."

"Huh?"

I slipped out of the dream and back into my own body. I felt the seat belt digging into my throat, the cold window glass against my temple, and a hand on my thigh. Blinking, I looked at the hand, then let my eyes follow the suit-clad arm to the shoulder, and the worried face waiting at the end. Mark.

"Yes," I said, pushing away from the window. "I'm awake."

He only nodded, that worry still etched in his forehead. I

didn't look at him but turned to the house instead. We were parked at the sidewalk, and the house stood big and empty above us, with windows like dark hollows ready to suck me in.

I suppressed a shiver.

"We could probably stay with Mrs. Hearth another night if you need it," Mark said, seeing my reaction.

I shook my head. "No. I need to go home sooner or later, might as well be now."

Mark didn't say anything, but I could feel the questions hanging in the air between us. Was this home now? Or would I come back with him to Toronto? What would happen to us if I stayed?

"Let's do this," I said and pushed open the door.

Mark was out of the car before I'd closed my door. Too quick, he was by my side, handing me the keys. I straightened my black skirt, shuddered within the black coat, before taking them. Still not able to look at him, I pulled at my skirt again.

Mark took my hand before I could reach for my hair and start patting it. "You're stalling."

I sighed. "Yeah."

"You don't –"

"Have to do this," I interrupted. Finally, I turned and looked him in the eye. "But I do, Mark. I really need to get over this fear. It... I can't be afraid to live in my own house." His lips tightened into a thin line and he glanced away. Pulling his hand from mine, he took off his glasses and started cleaning them, staring up into the bright October sky as he did so. "I know what you're thinking," I said, looking at my own hands and the dark polish on my nails. I'd started picking on it during mom's funeral, so parts were already missing. "But this is my home, it has always been, and I can't just walk away and let Connor win. I really can't."

Mark put on his glasses again and shook his head. "I know, but we need to talk."

"I know."

Without another word, I turned and headed up the path. Mark a few steps behind. I could feel his warmth there on one side, but a cold had crept up on the other.

"I think you're doing the right thing," aunt Ellie said, hovering just beside me. I could see her out of the corner of my eye. Like a grey fog. If I turned and looked straight at her, I would see a woman in her early twenties, dressed only in a blue bathing suit and with blond hair partly in a braid, partly flowing around her face as if she was underwater.

I didn't answer, just pushed the key into the lock.

The door swung open without a sound.

Aunt Ellie stepped inside, looking around as she walked. Mark pushed by me on the other side and walked straight through aunt Ellie's left side. She scowled after him, but couldn't reprimand him. I was the only one who could see or hear her, after all.

Taking a deep breath, I took a step into the house, and memories flooded me.

"You're going to die, Lizzie. You're going to die, and I will have killed you."... I did not want to get married. I wanted to run *"Free!" I yelled as I grabbed the banister to swing myself down the stairs like I had done so many times before... mom and dad fighting about something... me crying as dad held me in his arms, telling me he couldn't stay here, that he couldn't do this... mom smashing the pictures in the living room... a young aunt Ellie and a younger version of Connor, my father, sprinting through the house, laughing... someone playing an old violin, lulling a baby to sleep...*

*mother playing the piano, aunt Ellie by her side... mom screaming
as she attacked Lars, attacked me, attacked Mrs. Tav, killed me...
me lying beside her dead body...*

"Lizzie?"

I was flung back into my own body and my own head. Taking a step back, I bumped into someone. Hands gripped my shoulders to steady me.

"Sorry," I mumbled and pushed away from the body to stand on my own.

"No stress."

I recognized the voice and turned, a smile already moving across my lips. "Sara Hearth. What are you doing here?"

Sara grinned at me, and I took a moment to take her in. She was somewhere between one-hundred-sixty-five and one-hundred-seventy centimeters tall, with broad shoulders and a fitting chest. She wore a slim black dress that showed off her nice waist and shapely hips. Her hair was cut into a long pixie cut and died a dark green that made her blue eyes shine. She had a nose ring and multiple holes in her ears, and tattoos peaked out of the see-through arms on her dress.

"I always stay with grams on Samhain," I cocked my head at her, and she waved it away. "Halloween. Anyway, it's just 'round the corner, and with your mom and all..."

"Right, I saw you at the funeral."

"We just got back from the wake," she pointed over her shoulder and I saw Mrs. Hearth and her daughter, Abigail, standing at the porch on the other side of the street. A young man I hadn't seen before stood by their side, hands in suit pockets, looking at us. Abigail gave a small wave, and I lifted my hand in return. As soon as I'd done that, Mrs. Hearth grabbed both the man and her daughter and ushered them into the house.

"Emma would've loved to be here, but she's just had her baby," Sara continued.

"Yes, I understand."

We stood in silence for a moment. It was a comfortable one, the most comfortable silence I'd had in over a week.

I'd grown up with Sara and her older sister Emma. They visited Mrs. Hearth with their mother Abigail multiple times a year and stayed for a few days. When the girls were younger, they used to spend the nights at our place as Mrs. Hearth hosted some kind of party for the adult women of the family. When Emma turned thirteen years old, she was allowed to be at the parties. Both me and Sara were much younger than her, so we had a lot more time to bond, and we'd become fast friends.

"I just thought I'd check on you," Sara said now, bringing me back to the present. I could feel a small smile at the happy memories on my face. "You were just standing there, and I know you've been staying with grams since the accident."

"Yes," I said, smile gone again.

"So, you're ok?"

I glanced over my shoulder. Mark was nowhere in sight, but Eleanor, the oldest of my ghosts, was standing by the stairs, hands on her swollen belly. None of the others were visible, but I could hear low giggling from the floor above me. Probably the twins and little Magdalena playing.

"No, yeah, I really don't know."

"You wanna take a walk?"

"Yes, please."

Sara beamed, but my own smile died when I remembered Mark. "Just a sec," I murmured and stuck my head into the house again. "Mark?" I hollered.

"Yeah?" He answered from above, probably from my bed-room.

"I'm going out."

"Where?"

"Just out."

"Want me to come?"

"No."

Before he could argue, I closed the door and hurried down the steps after Sara.

2

"So who was the guy?" I asked as I buttoned my coat close against the chill wind sneaking down the street. "And aren't you cold?"

Sara only had a shawl thrown around her throat, but as we headed down my porch-steps' she pulled it out and wrapped it around herself. It was the same blue as her eyes, but looked muted compared to her hair, and reached from atop her shoulders and to her hips, hiding her torso within its softness.

"Nah," she answered, reaching one hand to me so I could feel the shawl. "It's alpaca wool, warm enough for this weather."

"Not for long?" I said with a wry smile on my lips.

She shuddered and laughed. "I never learned how to dress proper."

We walked past two houses and off the land my family owned before either of us said anything else.

"Really, who was the guy?" I asked again. "On the porch with your mom and grams?"

She smiled at her Doc Marten boots. "That's my boyfriend, Jake."

"I didn't know you had a boyfriend?"

She shrugged. "Haven't really advertised it, but we've lived together for over a year now."

"Congratulations."

"Didn't think I'd ever find a boyfriend, did you?"

I stiffened, afraid I'd somehow offended her, but when looking her way, I saw she was grinning that impish grin she'd used when we were kids and had done something we knew wasn't allowed.

I snorted. "Not with that attitude."

She laughed and took my hand, wrapping her fingers in-between mine and leaning against my side. "I've missed you," she said.

I leaned my head on top of her's and squeezed her hand. "Me too."

We walked to the end of the street in silence, holding hands and leaning on each other. I halfway thought Sara was just doing it for my warmth but knew she was trying to be there for me.

I was about to turn around and go back home, but Sara pulled me across the street and past the houses until we were one street over. Cuddling close to me again, she headed downward, eyes fixed on the playground at the bottom of the street.

"How're you doing?" she asked after a few steps.

A shudder tried to push its way through my skin but I suppressed it. "Fine, really," I answered.

"Don't believe you. Grams told me you haven't been home since it happened? That you've stayed with her?"

I glanced down at the top of her head. "What more did she tell you?"

Her hand tightened around mine for a second, and I wasn't sure if it was to reassure herself or me. When she answered, it was in a low voice, so no one other than me could hear. Not that there was anyone around to listen. "She told me 'bout the ghosts, and 'bout what really happened. Why Nancy attacked you. She told me you still have nightmares?"

Tears pricked behind my eyes at mom's name, but I forced them back down. I tried to speak but wasn't sure what to say. Ask if she believed me? If she thought I was crazy, like Mark?

Mrs. Hearth was a witch, or at least she claimed to be. She also claimed that all her family were witches, but I didn't know if that was true. Even with the ghosts tethered to a cold spot in my chest and the memories of the Red Woman and her grey world, I wasn't sure I believed it all.

Sara continued talking, "I'm so sorry you had to go through all that. I can't believe how scared you must've been. If mom had... I can't even wrap my mind 'round it."

"Do you believe me when I say she really believed I was someone else? That she was trying to protect me?"

We'd reached the playground and stopped in front of the gate, looking at the swings moving sluggishly in the wind and listening to the last leaves rattling on the trees.

"Tell me 'bout it?" Sara asked.

"Will you call me crazy?" I answered.

Sara pulled away and looked up at me. Her eyes were hard and sure. "No."

"Ok, then."

I pushed open the gate to the playground and walked in, letting her hand go. Sara was just behind me, closing the gate and sitting on a swing before I'd decided where to go. I sat on the other swing. We pushed back and forth for a time until our speed matched, then I started talking.

I told her about the things that had happened when I was younger. How Mrs. Hearth thought they were premonitions of danger. From there, the words just fell out of me.

I told her about how mom got out of the house and ended up attacking someone, how that was what brought me back home. The only thing that could bring me home again was her, after all, even if she was the one I was running from to begin with. I told her of the dreams that started when I got back home, about how a girl named Elizabeth died in each one. I told her about mom's ramblings and how she said I was going to die, and how the Red Woman had taken aunt Ellie, and now she would take me too. About how I started to think that mom maybe was crazy and had made up the Red Woman to hide the fact that she was the one to kill aunt Ellie. And how I thought that I was going mad because of my dreams and seeing this Red Woman myself. Then Mrs. Hearth told me I was a shaman, that the dreams I had now were just like the premonitions I had when I was a child, and that the Red Woman was really a dark witch that had cursed my father's bloodline.

Almost spitting in sudden rage, I told her about how I called Connor, my father, and how he didn't deny there was a curse. That he had known of it when he let mom name me after her dead best friend, Connor's sister, Elizabeth, my aunt Ellie. Then I told her that after he ran away from mom and me after mom got her Alzheimers diagnosis, he found a new woman and made a new daughter, a new family. How I was so afraid he would force mom to move out of his family home if I died.

And finally, I started talking about the ticking and that final day. How I brought Mark home for one last night of not feeling alone. About how mom was drugged and bound to the bed. About how I woke from a scream that wasn't the one in my dream, or even my own. I got to the point where I walked down the stairs and saw mom standing in the hallway, but I couldn't go on.

"That's when it happened?" Sara asked when I choked on tears. Our swings had stopped and she reached over and took my hand again. "When you died?"

Her words sent a shock through me. My ribs still hurt from the CPR Mrs. Tav, mom's night nurse, had performed to bring me back to life.

I nodded in answer and pushed at the tears streaking my cheek with my free hand.

"Grams told me a little of it. That you used your own power against the Red Woman?" I nodded again. "She didn't want to tell me everything. Said it was your story. Just said that what she'd thought proved to be the truth." She squeezed my hand and I turned to look at her. A sad but reassuring smile was on her face. "I'm here for you, you know? No matter what you need." I shook my head and looked away again.

When I didn't answer, she stood and walked behind me. Gripping both my hands with her own, she wrapped our arms around me, hugging me from the back, wrapping her shawl around us both so we shared warmth. I could feel her heart against my back, and I leaned into it, accepting the comfort.

3

We stayed like that until I stopped crying: me sitting on the swing, and Sara with her arms and shawl around me, breathing against the back of my ear.

"That must hurt," I sniffed when the tears settled.

"Nope," she said a little too quickly. "Not at all."

"I don't believe you. Stand up before you become all crooked."

She gave my temple a fast peck before standing with a groan. I could hear her back crack.

Drying my tears, I turned the swing and looked up at her. "We should probably get back before they start wondering where we are."

Sara shrugged. "Mine won't wonder. They know the two of us can take care of ourselves." She winked as she said it, and I blushed a little.

"Sure, but mine doesn't. He doesn't even know about you."

She feigned shock. "What? You don't talk 'bout me?"

I blushed again, this time with shame. Not for the first time, I was glad I had such a tan complexion that it hid most of the added color. "No," I said, looking at my shoes. Her Martens' looked clean compared to my well-used ballerina shoes. Most of my stuff was still in Toronto, so I'd had to use what Mrs.

Hearth and Mark could scare up from my closet here.

"Hey, don't worry 'bout it."

I sniffed again.

Sara grabbed my hands off the chains and walked with me around until the swing was the right way before she pulled me up. "Come on. We should get back. I'm starting to get cold and you need to eat. I watched you at the wake. You didn't touch nothing."

"I did."

"Like what?"

"I ate a shrimp and some salmon." And it made me both sick and craving more, but I didn't tell her that. Or that I'd completely lost the taste for meat this last week. Every time I tried eating it, I got these weird pictures in my head, like memories that weren't mine. I could only guess it was the memory of the meat I was eating, its life. Even the salmon and shrimp today had done the same. So why was I suddenly craving it now?

"That's not enough! No wonder you're just skin and bones. What happened to you? You're flat as a board!"

I scowled. "Why, thanks."

"You're welcome!"

She linked our arms and led me out of the playground. I could feel her wanting to ask something but not wanting to push. I didn't mind. The quiet was nice. Just walking like this with her was nice. As she'd said, we had a lot of history together, and it felt like we fell back into those days as we walked along now. I could almost smell the perfume I used back then. A shiver ran through me and I turned toward Sara, wanting to talk about something that wouldn't make me sad.

The words died in my throat and came out as a garbled shriek instead. I plunged back, pulling my arm from hers, and hit a fence, the poles digging into my back.

The Sara standing before me was a younger version. Her hair hung dyed black to below her shoulder blades with sharp bangs across her forehead. She had no tattoos on her naked arms, but a piercing in her lower lip. Her eyes, that had been mostly free from makeup, were almost swallowed by the heavy eyeliner and eye shadow. Her Doc Martens were dirty and well used, the same with her leather jacket, but her dark jeans were new, even if she'd drawn on them with a marker, and had buttons at the pockets.

"What?" Sara asked and the vision flickered.

"I..." I began but stuttered to a stop as I looked at my hands, afraid they'd be drawn on as I used to do as a teen. But no, my hands were clean except for the flaking nail polish and some dirt from the playground. "I thought I saw something."

"What?"

I only shook my head and continued walking. Sara jogged to catch up but didn't wrap her arm with mine again. Didn't touch me. Still, I could feel the worry oozing off of her.

We exited the short cut between houses and emerged on our own street. Mark was standing on the porch of my house, arms crossed and looking down the road. He wasn't wearing his suit jacket or tie. The setting sun shone in his glasses so I couldn't see his eyes, but his face was turned our way and he straightened from leaning against the wall when we came into view.

"That the bf?" Sara asked.

"If you mean boyfriend, then yes. Not so sure about best friend," I answered.

Sara made a face, but it was a friendly move.

We reached the curb in front of Mrs. Hearth's house and I moved to cross the street, but Sara grabbed my arm and pulled me into a hug before I could go. "If you need anyone to talk to 'bout anything, I'm staying 'til Samhain is over."

"Thanks." She booped my nose with her own as she pulled away, and I couldn't help but laugh. "Good to see you still have boundary issues."

She grinned. "Yep."

"And why can't you just call it Halloween like everyone else?"

"'cause it's so much more for us witches."

Before I could ask, she bounded up the drive and porch steps. As she opened the door, she turned and gave me a wink. Then she was gone.

Blinking, I turned and slowly walked across the street.

"Who was that?" Mark asked as I stepped through the ironwork gate.

I didn't answer before I was closer to the porch. "A childhood friend. Sara and I grew up together."

As I stepped onto the porch, he leaned in and gave my cheek a kiss. I forced a smile.

"You never mentioned her," he said as I opened the door.

I shrugged. "Never felt natural. How do you propose I would go about it? 'Hey, Mark, did I ever tell you about my friend Sara and all the things we ended up doing together?'"

He closed the door behind him. "Well, yeah. That's how most of my stories about growing up begin." I stepped out of my shoes and pulled off my coat. "Come to think of it; you've never told me much about anyone in your life, other than your mom."

He was rubbing his arms, and his nose and cheeks were red from the cold. How long had he stood outside waiting for me? I should care about the answer but didn't.

I shrugged and turned away, but stopped. Somewhere in the house, two children were laughing, and feet were tapping down the stairs. A blond girl dressed in a white nightgown was across the hallway before I had time to blink, leaving the house in silence.

I shivered.

"Lizzie?" Mark carefully touched me, and the heat of his fingers made me shiver even harder.

I pulled away. "I'm fine. It's just... being back here."

For a moment, I'd forgotten all the horrible things that happened to me in this house. I'd forgotten the fear and anger and sadness. Entering with Mark, talking about something small and trivial, had been so familiar I for a moment thought we were back in Toronto. But we were not. We were here.

Mark moved to hug me, but I stepped away again, almost unconsciously. When I realized what I'd done, his face was already drawn in hurt. "I'm really sorry," I said. "I just can't do this right now."

"Do what?"

"Ready or not, here I come!" A child's voice yelled above us, loud enough to make me jump and look up.

"Lizzie?" Mark again. My eyes flew to him but were pulled away almost at once by movement on the stairs. A young boy in old-style clothing came down the steps. He stopped when he saw me, put a finger over his mouth, then continued as quietly as he could, eyes searching the hall. "Lizzie?!" Mark grabbed my shoulders and I turned my face to him, blinking. "What is going on with you?"

I tried to pull away from him, but he didn't let me go. "I don't... I can't... You wouldn't understand."

"Try me."

"I can't!"

He sighed and let go. That hurt look was still on his face. "I don't know what we're doing here, Lizzie."

I clapped my hands over my ears, as if to block out his words, but I couldn't. "Don't call me that!"

All the little sounds of the house grew quiet. The steps I'd heard above. The rocking of the chair in the sunroom. The flipping of pages in the library.

When I opened my eyes, Mark was staring at me. Aunt Ellie came from the library, a blond girl in the nightgown, Magdalena, pressed to her side.

I turned back to Mark. "Don't call me that anymore."

"Call you what?"

"Lizzie."

"Why not?"

I wanted to cry and scream and claw at myself. Wanted all the feelings inside me to explode outwards for the world to see. Instead, my voice was steady when I spoke again. "Lizzie is dead. She died a week ago."

"What are you talking about?"

"I'm talking about mom, Mark. About the Red Woman and this house and my family. I'm talking about mom wrapping her hands around my throat and killing me, and what I saw when I was dead. What I did."

"I don't understand."

"And you can't."

"Why not? I can understand, you just have to help me."

"When I tried, you said I was hysterical and crazy and suicidal."

His face tightened, then he stepped toward me, moving his

arms as if to hug me, but I stepped back again. This time I hit the wall. He froze and grimaced. "Lizzie –"

He hadn't denied it. Not any of it. He thought me crazy back then and still did now. "Don't."

He knit his hands and let them fall to his side. "Fine. But, whatever I should call you, I can't do this alone. I've been trying, these last few days. I've been trying to be there for you, but you're just pushing me away. You won't let me touch you. You don't sleep. You don't eat. You won't even look me in the eye. What do you want me to do?"

The wall was hard and cold against my back. The floor cool and steady under my feet. My insides were a tornado of feelings and thoughts, but it was now or never.

"I need to figure some things out," I said, voice as steady as the foundations of the house around us. "I need to figure some things out, and I'm not sure you can be part of it."

"Wha –"

"I'm sorry," my voice broke a little. "But I need you to go. Go back to Toronto and go to school and hang with your friends. Live your life. But you can't do it here."

"I won't leave you like this."

"I want you to. Please, Mark. If you care for me, let me care for you. I'm not good for you anymore. I... Things are happening to me, and you can't help me with them, and I really don't want to pull you into this mess with me. It has ruined my life, and I don't want it to ruin yours."

He took another step toward me, and when I didn't flinch, he walked the rest of the way and wrapped me in his arms. "Whatever is going on, we can figure it out. Just give me a chance. Please, Li... please."

I closed my eyes and pulled in his scent. Honey and clean

clothes. His body was warm and I wanted to drown in it, but beneath that warmth was that small, cold spot inside of me. That spot connected to the ghosts standing by the stairs, looking at us. I could feel their eyes on me, could hear their breathing. Mark couldn't. He was familiar and they were not, but familiarity wasn't enough. Not anymore. Drawing another deep breath, I pushed him away as gently as I could.

"Please, leave me," I whispered.

"Don't do this," he answered, trying to meet my eyes but I wasn't looking at him.

"Lizzie is dead, Mark. The girl you fell for is dead. Please, just leave."

He stepped away from me then. His hands slid off my shoulders, leaving the skin there cold and tingling. I was still looking at his legs, and saw his hands knit at his sides. Saw his knees spasm before he moved. Sliding on his shoes, I heard him choke back a breath. Then the sound of keys jingling against wood. The door opened and closed, and Mark was gone.

I lifted my eyes. Saw the keys on the dresser by the door where he'd left them, saw all his clothes gone from the pegs against the wall. His shoes from the rack under it. He didn't have anything here. Everything he'd brought with him was at Mrs. Hearth's place.

He was gone, leaving me to the unknown.

"Oh, gods," I choked and fell to my knees, gasping for breath.

Aunt Ellie was suddenly there, wrapping her arms loosely around me so she wouldn't touch me, shushing and murmuring, trying to calm me.

"Why did I do that?" I asked, trying to lean against her but falling through her body instead. Hitting the floor, I dug my nails into the wood and screamed until my throat was raw from sorrow.

4

Darkness is here. So hungry. Can move now, so am sprinting. Sprinting as fast as can be. Hungry... Elizabeth was sitting in a chair, staring at the books on the shelves. Her fingers were fiddling with a lock of her blond hair as she listened to the voices of the twins as they played. Why was he so late? He should have been here by now. Mother had promised that there would be at least one suitor today. She... Can hear and see life but can't hurt it in this shape. Prey will have to wait. Need a body to hunt flesh. Know where to go. Can scent them. Scent the souls gathered at one spot, just waiting. Waiting to be prey... "I don't care what you think, Connor. There is no curse, and there is no reason for me to hang back and watch life go by." Aunt Ellie was flinging a messenger bag across her shoulder. "But please, Ellie, look!" Connor pushed the family bible toward her, the cover open and showing the family tree. Aunt Ellie pushed it away as she answered. "Life was hard back then. It isn't like that anymore. Now excuse me, but I've got a plain to... Sprinting. Sprinting and passing over ground frozen in sleep. Past human nests. Growling in irritation, even if they can't hear. Before, there weren't so many humans. Was a problem, for wasn't enough prey. Now, is too many. But no fear, they will be prey again. Just need a body. Will have a body... Sanderson was sitting in a nursery. The walls were painted a faint blue, like a winter sky, and stars were painted on the ceiling. A cradle stood in the corner, just waiting. Her hands rested on her belly, nails digging into her skin. She wanted to claw out what was inside and leave it. She didn't want this. She missed Martin. All she ever wanted was him. The baby kicked against her hand, and her heart jumped. Tears pushed up her throat and she curled around herself, crying quietly so her family wouldn't hear. She told herself she was crying for Martin, crying for the situation she was in, but deep down she knew she was crying because she really wanted to love this baby, but she was afraid it would make her forget... Scenting snow on air. Will come soon, and then prey will hide. No problem. Will still find prey, both flesh and soul, and eat. Sate hunger. Hunger. Hungry, so hungry!

I woke with the scent of snow in my nose and a growling stomach. Opening my eyes, I saw I was on the floor in the hallway, where I'd laid down after Mark left.

Mark. What had I done?

Pushing up, I made to move after him, but a flicker in the corner of my eye caught my attention.

Magdalena, the six-year-old ghost girl that died from falling down the stairs back in 1899, was sitting on the sofa, curled up against Eleanor, who was the first of us to be cursed. She died while giving birth to her son in 1743, but still had the big belly in ghost form. They were both looking at me. I looked back. If I looked closely, I could see through them. Not clearly, and you wouldn't notice unless you looked for it, but I knew and was looking.

The ghosts moved, as if aware of what I was doing and uncomfortable with the reminder.

Feelings stirred within me but I pushed them down, hard. I couldn't deal with them now. Just couldn't. Mark and mom and everything. This house. Sadness bit into my throat, but I managed to shake it off.

Without a word, I turned away from the door, pushed off my shoes and headed deeper into the house and toward the kitchen.

Picking up an apple, I washed it and bit into it, water still dripping from the green and yellow skin. Its juices were fresh and cold, despite the apple having been in a bowl on the counter. Even as I swallowed the first bite, I knew it wouldn't be filling.

I wanted steak. Even with the flashes and feelings coming with each bite. The thought of it made me want to gag; I wanted steak.

I continued eating my apple anyway, not in the mood to make a big dinner for myself. It would only go to waste. Even if I managed to make something appetizing, I'd probably not be able to eat it.

Sanderson came walking into the kitchen. Like Eleanor, Sanderson also died from giving birth, but unlike Eleanor, who died while her son was still inside her, Sanderson died after her son was born, so her stomach was much smaller. She'd died in a hospital in 1921, and was now pulling at the unflattering mint green hospital gown, like I'd so often seen her do. When a child's laughter came trickling from upstairs, she winced and gripped for her belly. It was still big, but not bursting-with-child-big. She'd died as soon as her son was born. Not like Eleanor that died just before her son was born and so still had a huge pregnancy belly. I'd noticed how Sanderson always stared at it when she thought no one was looking. I remembered the mixed feelings of love and sorrow from my dream and glanced away.

"Hi," I said after finishing the last bite of apple and moved to throw away the pit.

"So, you're talking to us now?" Sanderson asked, sitting at one of the chairs at the table that was pulled out. I didn't want to think about why it was pulled out. This house had mostly been left alone for the last week after mom died. Maybe she was the last living person to sit in that chair, maybe... "You in there?" Sanderson asked, leaning forward to catch my eye.

I shook my head and grabbed a paper towel. "Yeah, sorry. Just lost in thought."

"You know I was just joking, right? About you not talking to us? I understand it would be a problem if we started bothering you while you were around other living people. They'd think you ossified or something."

"Ossified?"

"You know, drunk on giggle water?"

Hearing her talking about alcohol like that made me want to laugh. Just thinking about getting drunk was both compelling and not at the moment. What would alcohol do with my powers? Would it make me see even more ghosts, or would it help tune them out?

I threw away the paper towel. "You can talk to me around Mrs. Hearth and her family. They know everything. I don't really know about that man, but Sara and Abigail and Mrs. Hearth know."

"Speaking of, Mrs. Hearth came to the door while you were passed out in the hall." I blinked at her. "She didn't want to enter unbidden, but she tried talking to you about Mark. When you didn't answer, she did something with her hands before she walked away."

"What kind of thing with her hands?"

"I don't know. Something heebie-jeebie."

I started biting at one of my nails but stopped before I could do any more damage. "Did her eyes glow?"

Sanderson shrugged. "I didn't look that close. We were curious, but didn't want to risk leaving you alone."

"Why?"

She shrugged again. "Just a feeling."

"Thanks, I guess," I said before yawning. "I think I'll go to bed."

Sanderson only nodded, not moving to stand from the chair, so I left her in the kitchen, still fiddling with her robe.

Eleanor was still on the living room sofa. Four other ghosts were gathered around her now. There was little Magdalena sitting as if glued to her side, and the nine-year-old twins, Jonathan and Johana, were sitting on the floor. Standing in the doorway between the library and the living room was the teen ghost of Elizabeth. The twins were Elizabeth's younger siblings, and they died together in a fire back in 1851. The fire burned down the current family home, and this Victorian was raised a respectful distance away from the burned earth, with a hope that it would be a happier place for the Key-family than the original mansion.

Now, Elizabeth's billowy dress and hair were moving faintly, as if in a breeze all of her own. I'd noticed it happened to the ghosts when they were feeling a lot, and I wondered what she was feeling now.

Aunt Ellie sat in the library, listening to the pregnant woman's story, but when she saw me, she stood and walked over.

"What's going on?" I asked in a low voice, nodding at the group before heading upstairs.

"Storytime. We started it in the Grey World. Us three adults would rotate telling stories," aunt Ellie said, walking beside me.

"Why?"

"It could be rather depressing just hanging around thinking about how we died or listening to that witch gloat about her curse."

I stopped. We were on the first landing. It was halfway up the stairs to the first floor. Someone had scrubbed Mark's blood off the wall and the clock where he'd hit his head, but I was seeing him fall down those stairs, pushed by mom. I heard the crunch as his head hit and could taste blood.

Turning away, I looked down on the ghosts, taking deep breaths to calm myself.

Sanderson was standing a little away, leaning around the door to look at the others. Her hands were gripping the gown so hard they were white, and her hair was moving in an invisible wind. When she noticed me looking, she gave a smile that didn't reach her eyes before walking into the room with the others. Eleanor greeted her warmly before she continued talking. None of the younger ghosts said anything, and I felt a pang of sorrow and pity for Sanderson.

Gripping the banister, I forced myself to lift one foot before another, and stepped onto the landing for the first time since that night.

Mark fell through me as if I wasn't there, and again I heard that crunch.

I closed my eyes and forced myself up the stairs, counting the steps. I'd grown up in this house, I knew how to move around not looking. My feet stopped just before I stepped onto the first floor.

I could feel aunt Ellie's uncertainty, but I didn't question her. Instead, I forced my eyes open and looked at the first floor-hall.

This was where mom had killed me, tried to kill both Mrs. Tav and Mark, and she'd ended up dying instead.

Out of nowhere, mom and Mark came flying. They grappled for a second just at the lip of the stairs before mom pushed him over and down. She disappeared in the same instance, and Mark fell through me and down until I heard the crunch of him hitting the wall and the clang from the clock being jostled. I winced, fighting myself not to turn and run.

Movement caught my eye and I saw mom bending over someone. It was me, I realized. Mom's hands were flying across my body, but it was blurry, as if I wasn't really there, which I was not. I was here, watching. Mom's mouth was moving, but I couldn't hear what she was saying. Her fingers formed to claws at my chest and she screamed into nothing. Then she shook and fell over, one hand still on my chest.

"I don't remember this," I said as Mrs. Tav materialized out of thin air and dragged mom aside, checking her pulse before checking mine and starting CPR as she gripped for her phone. "I was dead. How can I remember this?"

"You don't," aunt Ellie said, looking at the tableau with me. "These things aren't memories. Or, they are, but not yours. You can see ghosts. Some ghosts are souls, like us. Others are memories, like this."

"But how…"

"I grew up in this house as well. I remember seeing Magdalena's death every now and again."

"But my powers," I spat the last word. "Didn't come from your side of the family. Mom gave them to me."

"Yeah, but I was cursed. I had a link to Magdalena because of that, and so I would see her death at the foot of the stairs."

"How… I…"

"Nancy told me once that she heard crying and screaming at the same spot. I knew that was where Magdalena died but didn't dare tell her I saw it too. She also told me she felt and heard other things. Her powers weren't awake, like yours are now, meaning you will be able to see all the ghosts in this house and beyond."

"How do you know these things?"

"The witch. When she learned about you, on your naming day, she also learned what you could become. She hoped the ghosts of the world would drive you mad for her. When you grew up not seeing them, she started trying to kill you herself. She wanted you dead, so the line would die with you."

I stood still, staring at the spot where mom was no longer lying, dead. I could still see her by the wall, pushing me against it, choking me, but I couldn't bring myself to look directly. Mark came flying down the stairs, pushing her off me. They rolled along the floor, stopping just in front of us and grappled before Mark went over the edge and fell. Crunch, his head against the wall. My hoarse cry for mom to stop. Her gripping my throat again. Then I died, and mom started crying, understanding what she'd done.

This time, I saw a faint light form between the palm of her hand and my chest. Her hand was just above my heart.

Without thinking, I lay my hand at the same spot, feeling my heartbeat. Together with it, I felt a faint stirring. As if something asleep noticed my touch and wanted to be closer to it.

Sorrow bit into my throat again, and this time I couldn't keep the sob from escaping. Before it was all the way out, I turned and ran down the steps. I heard aunt Ellie call my name, and the voice in the living room died.

I passed by the group of ghosts gathered there without looking, and threw open the door, running into the cold October night on socked feet.

5

I was barely through the gate when the door on the house across the street flew open, and Mrs. Hearth stepped onto the porch, eyes on me.

I didn't know where I was supposed to run, but as I saw those worried eyes, I veered toward her and sprinted over the road, not looking or caring if any cars ran me over. Nothing stopped my flight, and I flew up the drive. Mrs. Hearth stepped from the porch and lifted her arms.

I almost fell into them, panting and crying, my body shaking as I gripped the back of her blouse and tried to melt into her. Her arms around me were warm and tight, hugging me, and she started to hum and rock gently back and forth. For every beat of her heart against my chest, calm dribbled through me until I felt empty and bone tired.

"Dearest Lizzie," Mrs. Hearth began but stopped when she noticed my wince at the name. "Dear girl, what happened?"

I shook my head. The picture of mom dying as she screamed over my body played before my eyes again and again, even if they were open and staring at the gloomy world around us.

"Do you want to stay with us for the night?"

I nodded against her chest, and Mrs. Hearth sighed. She'd stopped rocking and now gently peeled her arms away from me.

I stood straighter, but she kept an arm around my shoulders, even if she was shorter than me.

As she moved toward the porch, I saw Sara and Abigail standing in the doorway, the man behind them, unsure what to do.

"You ok?" Sara asked before we even reached them. Mrs. Hearth gave her a look that made her close her mouth and made me giggle. The only woman able to make Sara shut up was her grams.

"Why don't I make some tea?" Abigail said, and she disappeared toward the kitchen before anyone could speak up.

The scents of the house were warm and welcoming as Mrs. Hearth closed the door behind me, aunt Ellie barely managing to slip inside before it hit her. I didn't look at her and instead drew in the comfort of the home. I'd stayed here this last week, and the smells and feelings of the house were calming. I wondered if that was Mrs. Hearth's magic. Maybe that was how she knew I was in the street? I hadn't gotten around to asking her much about this new world I was suddenly part of after mom died. There was just too much else to do.

"Hey," the young man said as he reached out his hand. "I'm Jake." He was a little taller than me and skinny as a twig. It didn't look like he had any fat on his body, but not much muscle either. Compared to Mark's skinniness, Jake was fit. He filled out his body well. His dark brown hair was pushed up a little, and he had a somewhat lighter goatee and a faint shadow of beard on the rest of his jaw. His eyes were a muddy green with yellow dots, and they were big. Everything about him was sharp angles, but those eyes were soft. He wore a pair of suit pants and a pale blue shirt. It looked like he never got around to changing after the funeral.

I took his hand, mine shaking and cold in his big, warm one. It was callused as if he was used to working outside.

"I'm…" I stopped and blinked, staring at our hands. If I wasn't Lizzie anymore, who was I? Elizabeth? No, I couldn't be Elizabeth either. Not Ellie, that was aunt Ellie's name.

"Don't worry about it," Jake said, squeezing my hand. "I may have overheard that other guy saying something about you not liking your name anymore, so you don't have to give me one right now." He smiled, and I saw that one of his front teeth was chipped.

"'bout that," Sara said, linking her arm with mine as I let Jake's hand go. "What's going on with that boyfriend of yours? He left you? Now? Just say the word, and I'll find him and give him a beating."

"He didn't," I said, feeling calmer now than I had all day. "I left him."

"Why?"

"You don't have to answer that, dear," Mrs. Hearth said. She'd been standing back, letting me meet Jake and collect myself. Now, she stepped forward to stop Sara from her questioning. "I'm sure you had your reasons, and they are yours alone. Sara, don't bother her. Li… she's had a rough couple of days."

"I just asked," Sara sulked.

Thankfully, she didn't pull her arm from mine. Instead, she moved us into the living room, and we sank onto the sofa together. Jake took the other end of the sofa, sitting beside Sara, looking at us with a bemused smile.

Aunt Ellie followed but gave me as much space as she could without leaving me completely. For half a second, I wondered why the other ghosts hadn't followed, but I let it go almost as soon as I thought it.

Sara started talking with Jake, telling him a story about us growing up together. By the distance in his eyes, I guessed she'd told him this story before, even if she said Jake didn't know much about me. Even when not paying attention, though, he smiled and nodded in the right places. As Sara talked, Abigail came in with a tray filled with teacups, a kettle, and a bowl of Mrs. Hearth's homemade chocolates. Sara immediately grabbed a chocolate and started eating it as she spoke.

"Don't talk with your mouth full," Abigail chided.

Sara rolled her eyes but finished the chocolate before continuing the story.

All the while, Mrs. Hearth was looking at me. When the light hit her face just right, I could see her eyes shimmering yellow. A part of me wanted to shudder at the sight, remembering the Red Woman, but I was too calm. That was probably Mrs. Hearth's powers at work, which was also why her eyes were glowing.

I drank my tea and listened to them talk back and forth until I became aware of someone hissing my name. Turning, I saw aunt Ellie standing in the door leading to the library. She waved for me to come over.

Not wanting to interrupt the talking, I put down my half-empty cup and stood. My feet and hands were going a little numb from the tea, which was surprisingly pleasant and calming. When Mrs. Hearth moved to stand with me, I waved her back down and made my way to the sunroom.

Aunt Ellie didn't say anything as she stepped aside to let me through the door. There were plants everywhere. Most stood around in broad jars or hung from the beams in the ceiling. In the far corner was an extra glass cage that hosted what Mrs. Hearth used to call ''evil plants'' when we were younger. I asked her about it once, and she told me she collected poisonous plants that could kill just by a touch, so she had to lock them away. My eyes fell from the flora and found Eleanor, sitting in the rocking chair, pushing it carefully back and forth, Magdalena in her lap.

I blinked at the display for a moment before I closed the door so we could talk in peace. Or the others would think I was talking to myself. The moment the door clicked shut, Eleanor started rocking a little harder, the sound of the chair against the boards filling the room and echoing off the big windows for a moment. I wondered how she could move the chair but not doors. Could it be because of memories, like the scene back home? I suppressed a shiver. Sanderson stood and looked out those same windows, fiddling with her gown again. The twins and Elizabeth were nowhere in sight, but the threads connecting us told me they were back at the manor.

I yawned before I was able to voice my question, "What're you doing here?"

"We wondered what you wanted us to do," aunt Ellie said.

"What do you mean?" I sank down on a wicker chair. "Don't you sleep at night?"

Eleanor cleared her throat. "You know we don't."

"Oh, right. Well, do whatever you want, I guess. I'm staying here tonight."

"We guessed as much," aunt Ellie said. "Do you want us to stay here with you, or should we stay at the manor?"

Before I could answer, the door opened and Sara poked her head through. Her mouth was open, as if she was going to say something, but whatever it was never came out as she looked at the rocking chair. Eleanor stopped the movement in a heartbeat, but Sara had already seen. The sudden stop only made it weirder.

"Right," the witch said, drawing out the word and turning back to me. "Grams filled up your cup and wanted me to check if you're ok. Are you?"

I stifled another yawn and stood. "Yeah, I'm fine. Starting to get tired, really." I turned back to aunt Ellie. "Go back to the manor, please? I just... I don't want to deal with any more today."

Aunt Ellie nodded and motioned for the others to follow. She helped Magdalena down from the rocking chair and helped Eleanor to stand. But as the three of them went toward the door, Sanderson stayed put. I was almost out the sunroom door, Sara looking over my shoulder to see what I was looking at when Sanderson spoke.

"Lizzie?"

I stopped and cocked my head at her, too tired to argue about the name. The tea seemed to work just like alcohol: you didn't really feel it before you stood and moved around.

The ghost's hands were gone inside the twisted fabric of her gown and her eyes were on her naked feet. She opened her mouth, closed it again, furrowed her brow before shaking her head. "Never mind."

"Sanderson," I began, my voice both tired and questioning, but she shook her head and cut me off;

"Never mind. You didn't want to deal with anymore today anyway."

Before I could figure out what to say, she was jogging after the others, not looking back.

"What was that 'bout?" Sara asked. "Was that... some of your ghosts?"

I shook my own head. "Yeah. It was nothing important."

Sara said something about this being too weird, then led me back to the sofa and pushed the refilled, warm cup into my hands. I cradled it, feeling its warmth spread through my chilled body. I always felt cold these days. Like I was walking through a mist or something.

We sat in the living room for maybe an hour or so more. I ate a chocolate, desperate it would still the hunger, even as I knew it wouldn't. I didn't keep up with conversation at all, sipping my tea and yawning. I was almost asleep with my eyes open when Mrs. Hearth leaned forward and took the empty cup from my numb hands.

"I think it is time we go to bed," she said, moving to stand, but Sara pulled me to my feet.

"I'll take her," Sara said. "Emma's room, right?"

"Actually, she's been sleeping in your room, dear," Mrs. Hearth said, a smile on her lips.

Sara blinked a few times before grinning. "Fine, we'll just sleep there, all three of us."

Mrs. Hearth blushed. "That was not what I meant."

"Kidding." She was already pulling me toward the stairs. Jake stayed in the living room. He said something to the older women that made them both laugh and made Sara yell something over her shoulder, but I was too tired to listen.

Sara and Emma hadn't grown up in this house, but they were here so often that Mrs. Hearth ended up giving them their own rooms. She used them as guest rooms whenever someone else was staying over, but when the girls were there, they had first pick of the rooms. I was glad Sara hadn't arrived before today. I wasn't sure I could have handled being asked to move rooms until now.

On the first floor, my bag stood against the wall between Sara and Emma's rooms. Before I could say anything, Sara picked it up and shouldered the door to her room open. Two suitcases were on the floor, but she pushed them aside with her feet and let my bag fall on top of one of them.

"Grams changed the sheets earlier today, so they're clean. She was going to come over with your bag later, but after that Mark guy came flying in all angry like, and you didn't answer the door, she decided to wait 'till tomorrow. Guess that's a good thing."

I slumped down on the bed as she talked. It was a double bed, so it had been enough room for both Mark and me to sleep in this last week. It just hit me that I hadn't been alone since the first two nights I'd spent here when Mark was still in the hospital. Those nights had been horrible, as I kept waking from nightmares about what had happened, or I woke to the ghosts filling my bedroom. I'd woken Mrs. Hearth more than once by screaming, both in my sleep and awake.

Now I was going to be alone again, and I could feel anxiety move inside me, making my breathing shallow and burning away my tiredness.

"You look pale," Sara said and lay down on the bed beside me.

I rolled over so we were lying face to face, our legs curled up to our chest but feet still hanging off the side of the bed.

"I don't want to be alone," I admitted. I knew I'd sent my ghosts away, but their company wasn't the same as that of the living. "I've only spent two nights alone since... that night, and they were bad."

"'cording to grams, you don't sleep much at all?"

"No. I have nightmares. Some of that night, some... that are really weird. It feels like I'm someone else, somewhere else, you know? In dreams, you always know who everyone is, even if they are in the wrong body. In these dreams, I'm somewhere and someone else. Someone I don't know, and their thoughts scare me. When I can understand them."

"Understand them?"

"Some of them are in other languages. I can have a multitude of these dreams during one night or even during the day if I nap. They are always there, sometimes melting together. I'm so tired, but I don't dare sleep."

"Are all the dreams the same?"

"No. Or, some of them are kind of the same. It feels like I'm the same person, creature, in some of them. Some are just dreams. Me running around in the woods, or swimming deep underwater, or even flying. Some are something more in-between. Like I'm on fire or trapped in darkness or in light, and I know I should be afraid because I can't move on my own, but I also know I have nothing to fear. Then there are those where I do things I don't want to do. I... there's been some blood and killing in my dreams, or thoughts of it. A hunger for it. I... it really scares me because I don't know what they mean." I drew a deep breath and pulled my hands over my face, pressing my palms against my eyes for a moment. "But even when I'm just having the more normal dreams, I don't sleep well. It's like I'm truly awake and doing those things. Like I'm never really asleep, you know?"

Sara sucked her bottom lip into her mouth and started biting on it. She'd removed her makeup sometime between our walk and now, but her lips were still a soft pink.

"Have grams been allowed to work her magic on you?" I shook my head, feeling my hair knot between my skull and the duvet. "Ok, I'll go get her. Between the two of us, we should be able to keep your nightmares away for a few hours, but we gotta sleep too."

"How can you help?"

"'cause we're awesome."

Before I could ask any more, she stood and hurried out the door and down the stairs. I closed my eyes, my breathing calming and my body lightening. I was so tired.

I was …

…so hungry. Close now. Could smell them. Human nests all around. Some old, some new. Some of the old have spirit prey in them. If the cluster isn't enough, those prey will be enough. Can smell them, so close now.

Open mouth and roar. Just a spirit roar, flesh prey won't hear, but spirits will hear, spirits will know and fear.

The roar ripped through my head and throat as if trying to break me.

"Hey, calm down! Lizzie, hey!"

My eyes flew open and I was staring into Sara's blue ones. Someone was holding me, their arms wrapped tight around my torso so I could hardly move. Mrs. Hearth was at my feet, kneeling, holding my hands in hers and eyes closed in concentration.

"You back?" Sara asked.

I tried to nod, but her hands held my head in place, so I answered instead. "Yeah." My throat was raw, as if I'd been screaming. "What happened?"

Sara let my face go and stepped back. "I'd gotten downstairs when you started screaming. By the time we got here, you were thrashing 'round and hurting yourself." She pointed to my chest, and I looked down and got a glimpse of blood under my chin. "It's not so bad, just a scratch," she said when she saw the panic in my eyes. "But you wouldn't wake up."

A silence fell in the room. Abigail was standing in the doorway, her hands over her mouth. At that, I realized Jake must be the one holding me. I tried squirming a little, but his grip tightened.

"Sorry, I'm not letting you go before Mrs. Hearth tells me you're all right," he said, and I stopped.

What could he be thinking now? Seeing me trash and scream like that, then Mrs. Hearth kneeling at my feet like this? How weird must it all look to him?

"Don't worry," he said, his voice rumbling against my back. "I know what the Hearth's are."

I glanced at Sara, who just waved it away. Behind her, Abigail lowered her hands and looked away, her fear turning to annoyance. At my feet, Mrs. Hearth was moving. Finally, she opened her eyes.

"Mother? What did you find?" Abigail asked.

"There was something," Mrs. Hearth said, meeting my eyes as she pushed to her feet with a grimace. "But it is gone now. Whatever it was, it was hungry." At her words, my stomach growled, and everyone looked at it, even I. "And it is somehow affecting Lizzie."

I was too tired to ask her not to call me that. The fact that I still didn't know what I wanted anyone to call me didn't help.

"But it's gone now?" Sara asked. Mrs. Hearth nodded. "What does it want?"

"I don't –" Mrs. Hearth began, but I talked over her:

"Energy."

Everyone looked at me again, this time my face and not my stomach, and I met their eyes. I wiggled a little in Jake's arms. He let me go after a nod from Mrs. Hearth, and I scrambled off him until I stood in the middle of the room, the other people forming a triangle with me in the center.

"I was dreaming. I was inside something but it wasn't me," I continued, glancing at Sara, that gave a small nod. "It was running toward something. Something it wants to consume so it can get a flesh shape."

"A flesh shape?" Jake asked. He'd stood as well but hadn't

moved away from the bed.

"Yeah. It keeps thinking about how it can't hurt humans in its current form. It needs enough energy to create a body before it can hunt humans and everything else."

"Why?" Sara asked.

I shrugged. While the content of the dream was slipping away, I could still feel the hunger deep in my stomach, and the anger at the human pests who had flooded this world deep within my chest. It seemed to be melding with my own sorrow and hurt.

"Is this why you have trouble sleeping, dear?" Mrs. Hearth asked. "This is one of your nightmares?"

"It's a new one, but yes."

She straightened a little. "Ok. Sara wanted me to help you with it, and I think I can, why don't you lie back down?"

"What? What are you going to do?"

"We'll try to block whatever it is so you get some sleep," Sara said, glancing at her grandmother.

"It may be that it is affecting you this way because of how tired you are. You don't have any shields, so it can just waltz right in," Abigail said. She was picking at her bottom lip as she spoke, thinking.

"Abby, honey, why don't you and Jake go downstairs and make some sandwiches for me? I will have to stay up while we work."

Abigail nodded, still picking at her lip.

As Jake left the room, he bent and gave Sara a kiss on the cheek. She grinned at him until he was gone, leaving the door standing ajar.

Mrs. Hearth had been peeling back the blanket covering the bed until the duvet was exposed. "Take off your clothes and lay down, dear."

I did as she said, sitting on the bed to pull off my pantyhose. I was still in my funeral clothes, and suddenly I couldn't get out of them fast enough. I was thankful for the t-shirt Sara tossed onto the bed as I undressed.

"So how does Jake know about all this?" I asked, trying to think of something else than what was going on right now. My voice was a tone too high, afraid after the dream, not to mention the fact that I was lying down to let two witches work their magic on me. "Is he a witch as well?"

Sara crawled onto the bed, lying with her back against the wall, arms open and inviting. "There are no male witches," she said. "Now, come here."

"You going to spoon me?"

"I need to be as close as possible for my powers to work on you."

"What are they?"

Before Sara could answer, Mrs. Hearth cleared her throat. "We will answer your questions later, dear. Right now, we should concentrate on getting you a good night of sleep."

I wanted to ask more. There were so many things I didn't know about their world. I thought I'd known everything there was to know about Sara, but clearly, I was wrong, and I wanted to know what I'd missed. It helped me forget why I was sleeping in her bed instead of my own. Why I was in her arms instead of Mark's. Everything was so uncertain.

Before regret could get its grip on me again, I curled my back against Sara's chest. Her arms were warm and strong as she wrapped them around me and hugged me even closer. I could feel her heartbeat against my ribcage, making my own heart slow down to match.

Mrs. Hearth pulled the duvet over us, tucking us in like she used to do when we were kids and spent a night at her place, before sitting on the edge of the bed, stroking my hair.

The two women breathed in unison, as if they'd done this a million times before. I didn't know about Sara, but Mrs. Hearth had her eyes closed. I knew they would glow yellow when she started her magic. Maybe she closed her eyes to hide them? To spare me seeing the same kind of glow as I'd seen in the eyes of the woman that killed mom and me?

Before I could grab hold of the thought, a calmness settled over me. It was the smell of freshly baked cookies and fall rain and mom's paints. It was the taste of homemade pizza in my mouth, and the sound of the wind in the leaves, and mom humming. It was all the things that had ever calmed me in my life, and it seeped into my skin and roamed through my body with my blood until I was yawning and my eyes closed on their own.

This last week, when my eyes closed, I saw mom's face as she died. I expected the same to happen now, but it didn't. Instead, there was only blessed darkness. Not malevolent or dangerous, just the calm darkness of night.

With Sara's arms around me and the scents and sounds and feelings of the past and the present mixed with one another, I fell into a dreamless sleep for the first time in nearly a month.

7

I slipped out of sleep hours later when Mrs. Hearth moved.

"Shhhh, dear," she whispered as she stood, all but her eyes hidden by darkness. They were still glowing a faint yellow. "I need to sleep myself, and I am not sure if you will stay protected or not."

I tried to sit up, but Sara was still spooning me, holding me tight, and she didn't seem inclined to let go. Her breathing was calm and steady, and the scent of sleep hung in the air. I guessed Mrs. Hearth was the only one that stayed awake.

"What did you do?" I asked in an equally low whisper, staying still and looking up at her.

"My powers affect human moods. I kept you calm and tried to fight away the dark presence when it came."

"Did you win?"

The shadows on her face changed as she smiled. "Did you have any nightmares?"

"No."

"So I won."

I smiled at her happy tone, but it soon fell away. "So now what? Will it come back when you're not protecting me?"

"I don't know, dear, but Sara is still here and that may be enough."

"But how can her powers work if she's asleep?"

"She has to concentrate to turn off her power. I have to concentrate to turn it on. Every power is different."

"I don't –"

"Shhh," she bent and stroked my hair, the touch sending another wave of calm and tiredness through me. "Don't think about it now. Sleep. Rest."

I could probably fight it, the tiredness and calm, but it felt so good to relax like this that I didn't want to. With Mrs. Hearth still stroking my hair and sending waves of good feelings into me, I fell back to sleep.

So close. Could taste the energies of the spirits now. Could feel their feelings. Fear, resentment, sorrow. So hungry. Hunger would soon be sated. Soon. Human dens all around. Too late in the night for them now. All prey hiding in their hollows, hiding from predator. But some don't know to be afraid. The spirits don't know to fear for their lives. So stupid. The den holding the spirits is almost shining compared to the other dens (...home) Run up, ready to tear through wall of den (...my home) to get to prey within, but something is pushing back. Snarling, ripping at barriers. Like the Veil, but not as strong. Can reach it, can tear it all apart. Will hunt and grow strong! Hungry! (No! Stay away from my...)

"...house," I whispered as I woke.

A new silence filled the room, and I recognized it as the sudden silence of stopped conversations.

My eyes opened, and I turned.

I was alone in bed. Sara was no longer holding me.

"Lizzie?" Her voice came from the foot of the bed, and I turned toward it.

She was sitting at the edge, just a shadow in the gloom. Someone was sitting at her feet, hands in her lap. A man. Jake. I breathed out again, but before I could speak, Sara was crawling up the bed and lay down in front of me.

"It's ok," she shushed. "Just go back to sleep. I'm sorry I left you." I tried to speak, but my mind and body never truly woke up, and so I just lay there, looking into her eyes. They were glowing golden, like the sun through a thin cloud. "Just go back to sleep. Wish that you won't have nightmares, and my power will make it happen."

I blinked slowly at her, trying to understand what she meant. When I didn't close my eyes, she took my hands in hers and leaned her forehead against mine.

"Sleep." The word was spoken so softly I hardly heard it.

Closing my eyes, I wished with all my heart that I wouldn't dream of the hunger. That I wouldn't be part of that creature again.

The twins were running around, jumping on the sofas and scream-ing. I thought about joining them but did not dare. Mother and father had never liked me jumping on the furniture. They were not here, but I did not want to take the chance. I reached out my hand and...

...Magdalena Elizabeth's little hand snuck its way into mine and I turned to look down at her. Without a word, I lifted the six-year-old into my lap and wrapped my arms around her. We didn't speak, just sat and looked into nothing. I could feel her turn toward the twins, but I blocked out their screaming and yelling as best I could. Instead, I remembered growing up in this house. Remembered sitting just like Magdalena did now, but on my dad's lap, in this chair. It had been my favorite growing up, and it felt both weird and right that

Connor had kept it after I died. I...

... étais à la fois bénie et maudite par mon ventre. Je pouvais sentir mon enfant bouger en moi, même s'il était mort avec moi ce jour-là. J'avais la chance de me sentir encore enceinte, contrairement à cette chère Veuve Sanderson, qui avait perdu son mari et son enfant au moment de sa mort. Je l'ai vue regarder mon ventre avec envie, et je l'ai peinée comme seule une mère pouvait le faire. Je...

...couldn't stay in that house for another second. The twins were screaming and running around. Where was their big sister? Shouldn't she be there to calm them down? She was the reason they were dead, after all. But she had always escaped into herself, even in the Grey World, like the dewdropper she was. But that wasn't what hurt the most. Little Magdalena was staring at the twins with envy in her eyes. I had been there, standing beside her, ready to take her in my arms, when she reached for Ellie. Always Ellie or Eleanor, even the teen girl or the twins, never me. I longed to have her in my arms, as I longed to feel a child in my belly again.

No, I couldn't stay in that house for another second, so I walked through the back doors and into the garden.

The October night was chill and quiet. As a ghost, I could feel it and not feel it at the same time. It was a sad feeling to be standing beside the world in this way. We were frozen, and Lizzie was too much of a flapper to care about us.

I shook my head. No, that wasn't right. She was giving up her life for us, to help us move on. I respected her for what she was going through and how she handled it, but I didn't want to stay here longer than I had too. That wasn't an excuse for me to call her names, however. But the other women and children I was stuck with all reminded me of what I had lost, and I couldn't take the sorrow much longer.

Standing in the middle of the backyard, arms wrapped around myself, my hospital gown moving drowsily in imitation of the breeze touching the trees, I felt more alone than I ever had.

I almost didn't notice when my gown fell still around me, and when the chill no longer was a result of that standing–beside–the–world–feeling, but something as real as I was. But I did notice it, and when I did, I heard the sudden quiet of the night.

Even in a neighborhood like this, there were sounds. Dogs barking, cats mewling, a fox rummaging through someone's garbage, and night birds fluttering their wings. Everything was quiet, now, like it had been in the Grey World, and my stomach clenched in horror.

I didn't want to be alone.

Turning, I moved to enter the house again, but something caught my attention. A movement at the corner of the house. When I tried to look closer, I didn't see anything.

"Go inside, Liz," I said to myself. My voice sounding hollow and distant, as if that too was part of the real world. "You're just depressed because of everything, and you're seeing things. Maybe you should talk to the others, tell them what's going on with you? That might help. Now, get a wiggle on."

Still mumbling to myself, I turned toward the door.

My foot was barely lifted when something hit me from the side and bowled me over.

Before I hit the ground, something sharp bit into my neck, cutting off the scream that would have escaped otherwise. I was dead, I shouldn't be able to feel pain, but I felt pain now, and it flared through me like fire in my veins. The thing holding me sunk its claws into me, piercing both cloth and skin. Finally, I pushed out a whimper.

My own whimper woke me, and I scrambled to move. Sara woke

with a jolt before I was sitting up, having slept with her arms around me. Behind her, his arms around her waist, Jake woke as well. He was out of bed before either of us, asking what was going on, but I couldn't speak.

Pain was flaring in my throat and along my sides, like something was slashing me open, and I felt one of the cold strings starting to break. Something was happening to one of my ghosts.

8

Pain still blaring through me like venom, I pushed out of Sara's arms and past Jake's hands. My legs gave way when I tried to stand, and I tumbled to the floor with a cry of frustration and pain.

Sara's hands burned against my skin, but I let her help me to my feet before I pushed away and staggered out of the room.

Getting down the stairs was a trial of balance and determination. The pain was so bad my vision was blurred by tears, and I kept whimpering. All I wanted was to lie down and curl into myself and die, but I couldn't. Something was wrong.

Sara and Jake behind me, Abigail and Mrs. Hearth yelling from the floor above, I unlocked the front doors and stepped into the night.

The October chill hit my naked legs and arms, creeping into me and mixing with the venom coursing through my blood, and for a moment, I slipped out of myself and flew along the cold cord tethering the ghosts to me. I was lying on the ground. *Something huge and dark, see-through and real at the same time, sat on my stomach, hands deep in my chest. I tried to scream but had no voice left. I tried to struggle but had no energy left.*

It felt like I wasn't there anymore.

A scream splintered the air, and I was back in my own body

as I stumbled across the frost-slick asphalt. At the same time, I was on the ground, looking up at the thing. At the scream, it lifted its head, and what I saw kicked me right back into myself.

I stumbled, Sara or Jake catching me, but I was trying to run even as they helped me up, even as I felt claws wrap around my heart and pull.

One of the strings snapped, and the sudden emptiness of it was too much. I fell to my knees, weeping.

Sara, Jake, Mrs. Hearth and Abigail gathered around me, talking and trying to reach me, but I didn't hear them. Aunt Ellie ran through them and fell to her knees before me. I looked up into her eyes, so like mine, and saw that she was crying.

"What happened?" she asked.

"You don't know?" I croaked.

"Lizzie?" Abigail said, but I tuned her out. The rest of the living had gone quiet now.

Aunt Ellie shook her head. "There was a pain, and we felt you. We felt your pain, and we couldn't move, we..." her words trailed off.

"Sanderson is gone," I said, clutching at my chest where her cord had been.

"What?"

"Something killed her, something..." the creature flashed before my eyes and I started to shiver.

Mistaking my shivers for cold, someone wrapped a blanket around me and pulled me to my feet.

"Get the others," I told aunt Ellie, my voice hoarse and rushed. "Get the others and come to Mrs. Hearth's. Now. Don't be outside alone; try to stay together with us if you can."

My words were barely out of my mouth before she was gone.

As the hands on my shoulders turned me around and started

herding me back toward the house, I saw the rest of my ghosts spill through the locked front door of my home, down the steps and across the asphalt until they circled us.

I wanted to go back, to see what had become of Sanderson, but I knew she was dead. If the creature had attacked someone living, they would have died, but as it was, it only stole something from Sanderson. Her life energy, I guessed. Whatever kept her a spirit.

Hands directed me to the sofa in Mrs. Hearth's living room, and as soon as I was seated, someone started rubbing my wet feet and legs with a towel to bring back some of the lost heat. I just sat there, letting the Hearth-women take care of me as I relived Sanderson's death. Saw that creature again and again. Felt the emptiness deep inside me. She had wanted to talk to me about something. What was it? She'd seemed so unsure, so sad, and now I would never know. I would never be able to lift that sadness from her shoulders.

Someone wrapped my hands around a warm cup of tea before snapping their fingers in front of my face. I blinked and looked up.

The living were standing in a semicircle around me, looking at me with mixed worry and wonder. The dead were behind me. I didn't see them but I did feel them, prepared to protect me as best they could. Against what, I didn't know.

The fingers belonged to Mrs. Hearth, and when she finally got my attention, she sighed in relief.

"Now, dear, why don't you tell us what just happened?" she said as she sat in a chair, her eyes never leaving me. The others followed her example, sitting around the room, but all eyes were on me, and I realized they had no plans of letting me go back to bed before they knew what had happened.

I wanted to tell them but didn't know how, or even what to say.

As if reading my mind, Mrs. Hearth leaned forward a little, giving a small, reassuring smile. "Just tell us what happened, dear. You know we will not judge."

So I told them as best I could. About the dream, about the feelings, and about Sanderson.

When it came time to describe the beast, Jake asked me to wait and sprinted out of the room. He came back with a drawing pad and pencil case.

"Tell me what it looked like," he said, opening the case.

Did he want to draw? Now? What was wrong with him?

"Do it," Sara said, squeezing my hand.

Taking a deep breath, I told him what I remembered of the creature, the monster.

When I was done describing it and what I'd felt as it ripped out Sanderson's heart, we sat in silence. The only sound was Jake's pencil scraping across the paper. The sound was oddly comforting, for mom used to draw and paint a lot before she got sick. She usually used coal for her sketches, but while the smell was missing, at least the sound was somewhat the same.

Finally, Jake put down his pencil and turned the pad to me so I could look.

The creature was drawn from a lower vantage point, as I'd seen it through Sanderson's eyes, and I shivered, letting Sara wrap her arms around me in comfort.

On the page, what looked like a wolf skull stared at me with black hollows for eyes. Antlers sprang from its brow as if it was a deer, and dark fur started growing between the base of the antlers and stretched back and out of sight. Its shoulders were hunched and thin but covered in that same dark fur.

8

A drawing couldn't capture the feeling of malice and hunger that surrounded the creature, or the scent of it. Musky as if from an animal, bitter as if from blood, and sweet, as if from something decaying, but I still couldn't speak from fear.

"And this?" Jake asked, flipping the page to another one.

I hadn't seen much of the body, but I'd gotten a glimpse of one of its claws as it attacked Sanderson in my dream. The claw on the page fit perfectly. Not a paw as one would expect from an animal, but not a human hand either. The fingers, of which there were only four counting the thumb, were way too long for human hands and had an extra joint at the end. Claws seemed to make up most of the last joint. I hadn't said anything about fur on the claw, but Jake had added some of the rough fur at the back of the 'hand', but nothing on the fingers. It looked right, and I managed a nod.

"You know what it is?" Abigail asked.

For a moment I thought she was asking me, but then I saw she was looking at Jake, her jaw set in anger.

He was looking at his drawings again, flipping back and forth between them. "Maybe," he finally answered. "I have to ask Lizzie some more questions about its mentality, but I think that should wait until morning, don't you?" he looked up at me then, warmth, worry, and care in his eyes. "We could all need some rest."

I only nodded, not sure I could have answered any more questions about the creature, even if I wanted to. My mind was one big mess. I wasn't sure I dared go to sleep, either, but before I could say anything about it, the Hearth women were bundling me up to bed, talking over each other about how to keep my mind safe through the night.

When Sara lay down in bed again, arms around me, I started

weeping from exhaustion and sorrow and gratitude. I fell asleep crying, but didn't dream of the beast or any other deaths. The whole night, I dreamt I sat at the edge of my bed, looking down on myself sleeping in Sara's arms, her snoring softly. Little Magdalena had curled up against my stomach like a cat, and most of the other ghosts were standing around the room, keeping watch. Aunt Ellie was sitting on the edge of the bed, looking at me, love and worry brimming in her heart.

9

Humming drifted through my ears, and for a moment, I thought it was me doing it. But I was asleep, and I didn't even talk in my sleep, so how could I hum?

Opening my eyes, I blinked against the grey light that came through the window, the last pieces of sleep slipping away and leaving me with no memories of any dreams or nightmares.

Everything but the humming was gone. The sound coming through the door was familiar and alien all at once, and I suppressed a shudder.

I remembered going to sleep with Sara, but now the bed was empty except for me, and the smell of coffee and breakfast was sneaking its way up the stairs and through the open door. I also heard the soft voices of mostly women talking, every now and again interrupted by the rumble of a male voice.

I had to remember to thank Jake for letting me borrow his girlfriend last night. And ask him about him sleeping in the bed with us. It hadn't been a big deal last night, but now the thought made me blush.

The sudden heat in my cheeks burried the heaviness in my heart over last nights events, and I hurried to get up to find fresh clothes.

The room was cold, and I could feel my nose itch, a sneeze

on the way.

My ghosts were hovering in the hall. The three youngest sitting on a carpet, playing a hand game of some kind, singing in low voices:

''Lizzie Borden took an ax
And gave her mother forty whacks.
When she saw what she had done
She gave her father forty-one.''

When they reached the end of the verse, whoever it was that was next to slap another's hand had to do it fast, or they'd lose.

I watched as Johana missed at her brother. Jonathan and Magdalena both giggled as Johana got up with a pout, turned around and started counting. The two others sprang up and flew – literally – up and down the stairs to find a hiding place.

"How do I know that game?" I asked, turning to the other ghosts.

Aunt Ellie was in a chair, Eleanor was in another, and young Elizabeth was standing at the edge of the carpet where the kids had been playing, arms crossed and with a pout to challenge the one of her younger sister. If I didn't know any better, I'd guess the tween wanted to play with them, but she'd made it perfectly clear long ago that she was a lady and didn't play silly games.

She turned to me now, her pout falling away. "You have not played it?"

I suppressed a shiver. "A game about someone with my name killing her parents with an ax? No, I haven't."

"You do not know of Lizzie Borden?"

"No."

Elizabeth cocked her head, thinking. She hadn't made much out of herself in the week I'd known her, so I was happy she was finally starting to warm up to me. Maybe it was the shock of losing Sanderson.

"I think, perhaps, you know the game because we know the game." She pointed to her younger sister as Johana finished counting to one-hundred, spun around and raced toward the stairs. "Like you knew something was happening with Mrs. Sanderson yesterday. That we are linked."

She seemed to touch the cord between us and I could feel it thrum inside my chest.

"So, we are exchanging thoughts?" I asked and sneezed.

Elizabeth's eyes grew wide. "No... yes... I honestly do not know, miss."

"It's Lizzie," I said out of habit before remembering I didn't want to be called that anymore. "Anyway, who was Lizzie Borden?"

"An ungodly woman from Little Magdalena's time. She killed her parents with an ax and got away with it, from what I can gather."

"So why is there a game about her?"

Elizabeth paled a little and looked away, and I instantly regretted asking, as if I'd scared her back into her shell.

"There wasn't much for us to do in Limbo," aunt Ellie said. "We exchanged stories, built on our own knowledge, and made games. Even if we couldn't move, making up the games seemed to calm the youngest when they were scared," as she said this last, her eyes flickered to Elizabeth, who was still only a tween herself. She must have been more scared than anyone, after bringing her siblings into that world.

"So, if I know what you know, why don't I remember every-thing about your lives, but know this song?" I asked.

This time, I couldn't suppress the shiver, and Elizabeth gave me a sympathetic look. As if she knew what I was thinking.

"*Peut-être* you have to experience it to remember it," Eleanor said, and as I listened to her French accent and remembered the dream in which I suddenly thought in French, I also knew she had kept the accent on purpose while in the Grey World. It was a link to the life she didn't want to let go, even if she could speak perfect, if aristocratic, English now.

As the realization hit me, I saw that she knew that I knew. With a sigh that made my bones heavy, I walked past the ghosts and into the bathroom. Thankfully, they didn't follow.

I did my morning rituals before heading downstairs. Johana had found the others by now, and they were all waiting for me in the hallway outside the bathroom. When I walked down the stairs, they trailed after me, like a light river.

The voices in the kitchen grew quiet as I passed and headed toward the front door. Part of me wanted to enter the kitchen and eat something, anything, but again the mere thought of it made my stomach churn unhappily.

"Dear?" Mrs. Hearth asked, coming out of the kitchen to see what I was doing. I partly turned to her as I started dressing. "Where are you going?"

I sniffed, trying to clear my clogged nose before answering: "I need to see what really happened yesterday. I need to see if Sanderson is still there."

Mrs. Hearth looked into the kitchen like she expected this, and Jake came out from behind her.

"I'll go with you," he said.

"Why?" I asked, stopping in winding my scarf around my throat.

"I want to see if there is anything for me to learn there." I sneezed again, which made him smile. "And in case you get sick and need carrying back."

This last he said with a smile. I wanted to ask him more, but couldn't really be bothered. I didn't even know what I was looking for. Maybe Jake, whatever he was, did.

Before we could leave, Mrs. Hearth pushed travel mugs of warm tea into our hands. "You will drink that," she said to me, her voice as stern as if I was a child and she'd caught me trying to sneak out. "I will not let you get sick now."

I grumbled a thanks from within my scarf, which she tightened and tucked into my jacket before she opened the door for us. Jake and I stepped out on the porch, my ghosts close at my back.

Maybe there was something to what Elizabeth had said, for I could feel their understanding of what I needed to do, as well as their curiosity about Jake all jumbled up with the sorrow about Sanderson. Or maybe that was just my own feelings.

"So," I asked as we stepped onto the curb. "Why do you really think there is something for you to see there?"

He took a sip of his tea – or was that coffee? Maybe Mrs. Hearth had only given me tea. I sipped my cup. Yep, tea, and an herbal blend at that, probably homemade. It was spicy and seemed to clear my nose instantly. If nothing else, that woman knew how to make me feel better.

"I'm a chronicler," Jake said. "'tis what I do."

"A what?"

We stepped onto the curb on the other side of the street and I stopped, staring up at my house. Jake reached the gate before he realized I wasn't following, so he came back. We stood there, side by side, drinking from our mugs and looking at the house.

"A chronicler," he said now, content to just stand there and talk, thankfully. "Or a witch's son, you pick."

"I thought witches bred true?" I asked, remembering Mrs. Hearth talk about shamans and witches back when I thought I was going crazy or getting sick. "And that there were no male witches?" Sara had said so last night, hadn't she?

"Well, yes and no. Witch's sons are the exception to the rule, one could say. We come around rarely, most witch families have never had a son at all. I only know of three others here in Canada, and one of them is my mentor."

"So, there's like one son born every second or third generation so the previous one can be the next one's mentor?"

He huffed a laugh. "Something like that. I guess when old man Johnson dies, I can expect a call from some angry witch telling me I'll get an apprentice in a year's time."

We stood for a moment, drinking from our mugs. The warmth and spices did wonders for my clogged nose and the weak shivers I wasn't sure were fear or cold. The ghosts swirled around us. Impatient and curious, scared and sad all at once.

"So, one year? Does that mean you were sent to this Johnson guy when you were just born?" I finally asked.

"Yeah. Sons don't grow up with the coven we're born into. We know all the rituals and spells and stories, but we aren't part of any coven." He laughed. "The fact that Sara and I are dating... you should have seen the faces of some of the older witches at that one. A witch's son has never, as far as our history knows, married and made children with a witch. They have sometimes married and bred with normal human women or other lines of magic, but the offspring never has anything of the father's powers. With a witch, though? Who knows."

I glanced at him. "Is that the only reason you're dating Sara? To figure out what will happen if the two of you 'breed'?" I snarled the last word as if it were a curse.

He huffed that laugh again. "No. Sara and I... We found each other when we needed it most. We are best friends and more. Even if we broke up, I think we'd stay best friends. Her powers... they can corrupt her, and many witches shun her because of it."

"How?"

"That's her story to tell."

"Do you have any powers?"

"Only passive. I can brew potions and cast ritual spells, but I don't have the personal power all female witches are born with."

"So what do you do? Why are you called chroniclers?"

"We write down the history and lore of our kind. The only personal power we have is our memory. 'tis a collective one, so if I need to know something I personally haven't read or discovered, I can tap into the collective memory and shift through them like a book until I find what I need."

"That's... really pretty handy." I couldn't help think about how that could have made things easier for me in high school.

"Both yes and no. We don't serve much else of a purpose. Witches use us for our knowledge. Has someone tried this spell before? What did they use? How did it go? What do you think could have gone differently? A few use us as storytellers. Inviting us to their daughter's birthdays to tell stories of dark witches and how to avoid becoming one, and the like." He looked at me. "Mrs. Hearth reached out to me about your Red Woman, but none knew much about her. All I know is that she left her coven behind in Scotland and wanted to start a new one here, some kind of falling out with her sisters and mother, and then was cheated by the man she hoped could make that a reality."

I was shivering openly now, clutching the mug with both hands to try to stop it. Elizabeth and aunt Ellie were talking to me in low voices, trying to calm me as the memory of the woman that cursed my family and killed my mother flashed through my mind like a film in fast forward. All the nightmares. All the fear. And now the sorrow.

"Hey," Jake reached out, cupping my hands with one of his own. "I'm sorry I brought it up. 'tis just annoying that I couldn't help, and I felt even worse when I learned how it... ended." His eyes flashed to my house. "I'm sorry."

"No," I managed between breaths. "It's ok." My hands had stopped shaking and I downed the last of the tea. "I can tell you about her sometime, if you want, at least what I know and what happened, so you can add her to your memory."

He beamed, even as remorse clouded his eyes. "I would appreciate that, thank you."

"So," I said as I turned away. "Why did you tell me all this?"

He shrugged. "You asked, and you know about the Hearth's, and I know you are something, so why not."

"Know I am something?"

"Yes. I have my suspicions, but I'm not sure yet."

"You want me to tell you what we think?"

"No. I like a mystery." His eyes sparkled. "You emptied your mug?" I nodded. "Here," he reached out and I gave it to him and watched as he sat it carefully down in his messenger bag. "Shall we do this?"

"Yes," I breathed and walked toward the driveway.

10

We didn't enter the house but followed the driveway toward the back, and we didn't speak as we walked along with the house and stepped off the asphalt and onto autumn-browned grass to walk around the garage. Fear had started to gnaw at my belly again, or maybe it was hunger. Feelings I couldn't yet identify were swimming through my blood and seemed to grow stronger for every step.

Rounding the corner of the garage, the garden came into view and the feelings rose from my blood and hit me in the face. I stumbled, barely feeling Jake's hands on me as he kept me from falling, as fear and pain and hunger and satisfaction and regret and grief swarmed through me. In the deep of my mind, I could hear Sanderson screaming, even if she never had the chance to do so before disappearing from this world for good.

Jake's voice whispered through the scream, and I was able to turn my face toward him. His brow was furrowed and his lips were pale. "What's going on?"

As he spoke, he glanced around. As if he could see the ghosts that were swarming around me, crying and screaming in their own agony, trying to comfort me as well as themselves.

I closed my eyes, choked back tears and tried to think despite the scream.

"Sanderson," I managed to say. "She died here," for every word spoken, the next came easier, grounding me to my own body and not in the feelings of my ghosts. "That was what happened last night. Sanderson was killed." Her scream was barely a whisper now, one I felt bad for pushing back, but had to if I wanted to get a closer look at what had happened.

"So you were overcome by sorrow?" While his face was worried, his voice seemed dubious.

I opened and closed my mouth a few times before I was able to put to words what I was thinking. "Yes and no. There's my sorrow for what happened and that I couldn't stop it, but there was also all the other... feelings."

"Other feelings?"

"Everything Sanderson felt just before and after the attack, and the feelings of the thing that attacked her."

Jake took a step back from me, but it didn't seem to be in fear. More like he wanted to be able to take in all of me with one look. His eyes were running up and down me now.

"How can you sense that?" he finally asked.

I opened my mouth but couldn't answer, so I turned toward my ghosts. As I calmed down, so did they. They were huddling together by the fence, as far away from the backyard as they could get without leaving the plot. Magdalena and Elizabeth were crying. Both cradled in Eleanor's arms. Elizabeth was holding the twins, much as she had on the day they died. A flash of fear ran through me at the memory and I felt the fire licking hot against my skin before it disappeared as fast as it came. When I blinked, Elizabeth, Jonathan and Johana were looking at me with unreadable expressions in their eyes.

Shaking my head, I was able to ask what I'd originally thought of. "How can I sense what they felt?"

Jake furrowed his brow and opened his mouth before he realized I wasn't talking to him. He turned to look, but couldn't see the gaggle of ghosts.

Aunt Ellie, standing with one arm around the weeping Eleanor, was the one to answer. "I guess it's like the memories inside the house. The ghost of the feelings remain."

"But how come I don't sense feelings everywhere I go?"

"Maybe because you were linked to Sanderson? We don't know, Lizzie. This is as new to us as it is to you."

"Hardly," I mumbled, forcing myself to turn toward the garden. "You've all been dead longer than I've been alive." The look on Jake's face almost made me smile. Almost. "I can't really explain how I feel it," I told him. "Not right now."

After a long pause, Jake nodded. "Later, then?"

"Later."

And with that, I couldn't stall any longer and forced myself to look at the backyard.

The feelings and screams were still there, but having been planted firmly back into myself, I managed to keep it at a distance for now.

At least until I was shocked at what I saw, then the feelings came roaring back, but I managed to push them away before they could consume me yet again. I wasn't even aware that I'd taken hold of Jake's hand before I was back in control. As soon as I realized, I let him go.

He was looking both puzzled and worried.

Lifting my foot, I took a step into the backyard.

The grass was the natural brown of autumn, littered with leaves I never got around to raking away. It was still early morning, the sun partly hidden by thin shadows and covering most of the yard in fall gloom, but even in this weak light, I saw the area where Sanderson had died.

It was black. Not brown like the rest of the lawn, or the greyish dark of the western sky, but black.

Nearing it, the scream grew in my mind and I could feel the rest of my ghosts trying to pull away from it. Something moved in my chest as if stirring awake.

I stopped just at the edge of the blackness.

The center of it was pushed down into the dirt as if a massive weight had been upon it, and I could see the shape of a body. There were grooves in the dirt where Sanderson had dug her nails into it, trying to claw her way out from under the creature, and a fleeting thought went to how a ghost could do that, but it was swallowed by the scream before I could pursue it. The black spread out from the human shape, twisted as it was, reaching like tendrils some places and spilling like a pool in others. No memory played out and I could have sobbed in relief. Just the thought of living through that again made me shiver.

"By all the knowledge in the world," Jake said in a hushed voice beside me.

I jumped, having forgotten he was there.

"Do you know what this is?" I asked, turning away from the black and looking at him.

He circled the black shape, taking care not to step on any of the pools or tendrils as he moved. "Something sucked the life right out of this area."

"Not an area. It was a woman."

He stopped at my words, standing on the other side of the blackness now, looking across it. "A woman?"

"Yes. See the shape?" I pointed it out to him. Where Sanderson's arms had been flailing. Where her legs had scuffed at the leaves before finally going still. Where her torso had been pushed deep into the earth and where her head had flattened the grass.

A light shimmered within Jake's eyes when he saw. "I didn't notice," he said in a low voice. "I can barely see it. This woman, she was how you knew what was going on? This was Sanderson, right? The one you were screaming for last night?" I nodded and he lifted his eyes to meet mine. "What was she?"

"Wha –"

He waved his hands as if saying he was sorry but not able to contain his enthusiasm. "You talked to someone invisible earlier. You said they'd been dead longer than you'd been alive. You can see and talk to ghosts all the time, can't you? This Sanderson... was she a ghost?" I nodded. "Fascinating." He was pulling out a pad and pencil from his bag and started sketching the blackness. "So the creature attacked a ghost and ate its energy, then somehow tapped into our plane and started sucking life from the very ground on which it stood. That is how the ghost could affect the grass as well. That is absolutely fascinating."

I turned and looked at aunt Ellie, who was still huddled with the other ghosts by the fence but looked as puzzled and angry as I felt. The older members of my ghost group had stopped crying and were looking on in mixed horror and intrigue, just like humans would slow to look at a car crash, I realized.

"So what do you think did this?" I asked, turning back to Jake.

"I think... no, I don't want to say yet."

"Why not?"

"I might be wrong."

"How can you be wrong? We have a picture of its face, of its hands, and we know how it kills. We know how it thinks, how it feels," I shuddered at giving the creature feelings. "We know what it wants. How can you not know what it is?"

Sighing, Jake looked up from his sketch. "Because something like this hasn't been seen on our plane since the Veil was created."

"The veil?"

"You really don't know anything, do you?" I puffed up my cheeks, angry and offended, but he shook his head before I could answer. "Sorry. Mrs. Hearth told me about your mother and her history. Other than what Mrs. Hearth could tell you when she was unsure of what you were, there is no chance of you having learned our history. I'm sorry I implied you didn't know anything."

I let out a huff of angry air. "So now what?"

"I need to finish sketching this. Could you look around for anything else the creature left behind? If it can affect spirits, it isn't quite on our plane, and so it may leave tracks I can't see but you can."

"Why?"

His eyes twinkled. "You're a shaman, aren't you?"

"Yes."

"I knew it!"

A surge of something moved through my stomach, and before I had thought of the words, they spilled out. "Can you help me? Help me help my ghosts, I mean?" I don't know why I didn't ask him before, but that didn't matter. He'd figured it out, so he could help me. Right?

The twinkle in his eyes died. "I'm sorry, I can't."

The surge shrunk away. "Why not?"

"I don't know enough about it. I've never met a shaman before, and even with the knowledge I possess, I don't know anything about their rituals or how they work."

Discouraged, I looked on as Jake returned to his sketching, moving around the black area to get it all. Sometimes, he would glance up at me, and I saw the pity in his eyes. The sadness for not being able to help. It didn't do anything to drown out the feeling of helplessness moving through me. To get away from the thoughts, I wondered why he didn't just take a photo with his phone, but as he'd pointed out, I hardly knew anything about this world and I didn't want to seem more ignorant than I already was.

Finally, I turned away from him and started looking around the yard.

We'd been at it for about half an hour and my nose was starting to get stuffy again and we hadn't found anything else than the black spot, when a car pulled into the driveway, its light both illuminating and going through the ghosts that had finally relaxed enough for the oldest to help me look for clues.

Jake had finished drawing the darkness and had taken pictures with his phone, before he stared blankly into space, chewing on his bottom lip every now and again, and furrowing his brow. At the sound of the car, he blinked and looked toward the driveway.

"Who's that?" he asked.

I shrugged. I wasn't expecting anyone. Maybe Mark was back? The thought sent a shiver of mixed fear and joy through me. I was both sad and glad he hadn't reached out yet. His showing up might make things easier for both of us even if I didn't know what to say to him.

A smile was already forming on my face as I rounded the corner of the house, but a feeling of sadness and anger and love and disappointment thrummed along the line connecting me to aunt Ellie, and even before I saw the car, I knew who it was.

11

The car was a sleek, shining, black BMW. Probably a newer model. Connor, my father, was exiting the driver's side door as I stopped in the small opening between the high stone fence and the garage wall, staring at him.

He hadn't changed much since I saw him last. His hairline had pulled back at the temples, giving him a subtle hint of horns. His hair was naturally ash blond, so the grey was well hidden. And he'd gotten more of a belly.

"Dad," I whispered before reminding myself that he lost the right to be called that by me a long time ago.

Still, a small part of me wanted to rush forward and into his arms. Wanted to bury my nose against his chest and pull in that scent I'd grown up with. That part was the girl I used to be. The girl that fell asleep on his lap as he read her Harry Potter or told one of the many stories he had about his family. The teen that said she hated him and didn't mean it but knew she could say it because he would always be there. He would always be her dad, after all.

That small part of me grew still as I locked it away and glared at the man. He hadn't always been there. He left.

"What are you doing here?" I asked, loud enough for him to hear.

On the passenger side of the car, the door opened and an Asian woman stepped out. Her skin had the golden tinge of the Thai people, and her eyes were big and dark with a weak tilt. Her hair hung black and shining to her waist in a loose ponytail. She was shorter than mom had been, shorter than me, but other than that, mom and this woman, Catherina, looked much alike. The long, straight dark hair. The wide jaw and lips. Mom's lips had been long and full, while Catherina's were more of a cupid's bow.

"I wanted to show my respects," Connor said, dragging my attention back to him.

"You're too late. The funeral was yesterday."

He was walking around the car now, closer to me. "I remember a certain someone telling me I wasn't welcome to the funeral."

I growled. "That someone told you you weren't welcome back here at all."

He stopped in front of me, looking me square in the eye. We were of almost the same height, him just a little taller than me.

"That is not a choice you can make. This is my childhood home as much as yours." Before I could say anything, he turned away from me and looked at Jake. "And you must be Mark, a pleasure. I'm Connor Sebastian Key."

Thankfully, Jake didn't take his hand. "No, I'm not. Lizzie, should we go?"

I didn't acknowledge him but marched past Connor, making sure to bump his shoulder as I did, and headed toward the street.

"Where are you going?" Connor called after me.

I glanced at Catherina, who had just lifted their infant daughter out of the car and was cradling her in her arms. The woman gave a nervous smile as our eyes met.

A small part of me wanted to smile back, but I pushed it down.

"Back to Mrs. Hearth," I answered, turning fully around and walking backward. "By the way, do you have a room in town?"

Connor was walking down the drive, hands in his pockets and as relaxed as could be. "Now, why would I do that when I have a home waiting for me?"

I couldn't help the angry smile pulling at my lips. "We changed the locks after you left, so good luck getting in."

I turned around again as my feet hit the curb, glad I hadn't stumbled. Jake was by my side, his eyes jumping between my face and the door to Mrs. Hearth's house. I could see the curtains pulled aside on the front window and the three generations of women looking out on us.

Hurried steps sounded behind me and before I was in the middle of the street, Connor grabbed my arm and turned me around.

"Hey!" Jake yelled, having been pushed aside by the motion, but Connor didn't seem to hear him. He stood way too close to me, pushing into my personal space the way he did when he yelled at me when I was a kid, trying to intimidate me.

"You had no right to do that," he said, voice even and calm. The calm of true anger. "Some of those locks were original –"

"Why shouldn't I?" I cut him off before he could start talking about his darling antiques. "You weren't here. I needed a lock mom didn't know how to bypass when she started to sneak out at night. It was only natural."

"And still she got out, isn't that right?"

Something stirred in my chest. Something with claws. "What? Have you been keeping tabs on us?"

"You are my daughter."

I finally pulled my arm free, feeling anger and sorrow war

for attention inside me. Feeling the cold spot in my chest grow as the claws that usually held it in place flexed and moved and pushed. "You have no right to call me that. Not after what you did." My own voice was as cold as his. I'd learned from the best, after all.

"And what did I do?"

"You. Left."

His anger seemed to melt away and he slumped, taking a step back. I blinked in surprise. This had never happened before, when he was angry, he could stay that way for hours, even days.

Connor heaved a sigh. "I know. But, Lizzie, you have to understand, I needed to get away. I couldn't deal with what was happening. I needed time to think."

The anger that had wavered at his retreat flared up again, and the thing inside me pushed harder. I could feel it against the skin of my chest now. Feel the tickle of feathers as it breathed and moved.

"You couldn't deal with it? Really? So you left your teenaged daughter to handle it? Then you went and got a new family?" I was yelling now, not able to keep my cool any longer. Anger was spilling across the strings connecting me to the ghosts as well, merging with aunt Ellie's disappointment and sorrow. There were too many feelings. "Yeah, don't think I haven't noticed how she looks like mom!" I was pointing at Catherina now. The woman took a step back, hitting the side-view mirror with her rump. "And then you have the nerve to show up here and try to act as if everything is normal the day after I've buried her? Really?"

"Come now," Connor said. I'd seen the anger moving over his face as I spoke, but he tried to stay soft and calm. Not the angry calm, but the calm one might use with a hysterical woman. I'd seen him do it before. And I realized Mark had been acting the same way toward me lately. "Why don't we go inside and talk about this? I'm sure you just need to relax and have a good cry and –"

His hands neared my shoulders, as if to comfort, but I cut him off with everything I had.

"Don't touch me!"

The words flew from my mouth as a white owl flew from my chest. It hit Connor just below the ribs, making him fly backward before the owl spiraled up to the sky.

Both Jake and Catherina were screaming something. Cornelia, the baby, started to cry at her mother's shock. Connor was sitting on the asphalt, gripping his chest as he tried to draw the breath that was knocked out of him.

"Don't you dare think you can just come back like this and we can continue as if nothing happened," I hissed, feeling the anger reach out of me, through the ghosts, and into the world. I wanted to hurt the man before me as he had hurt me. "For it happened. You left me, and things have changed. I have changed."

At those words, he managed to draw a breath and look up at me. His eyes were wide with terror as the ghosts drew closer around him. I could feel the emotions rolling off them like they were amplifying my own need to hurt him, and it scared him. My anger had reached other spots of cold out there as well. I could feel them like beacons in my mind, and for every one I touched, another cord was added to the spot in my chest. With every cord, the amplification of my anger and hurt grew stronger, until one could hardly breathe the air around me without choking on it.

Connor was trying to get up, but my gaggle of ghosts had

closed around him and was somehow holding him down, pushing the breath from him, replacing it with fear.

"Enough!" Jake grabbed my arm and turned me around. "Stop this."

His words broke through the haze filling my head. It felt like a slap as something snapped shut inside my mind.

The owl landed on my shoulder and buried its beak in my hair, as if to comfort. The terror was gone, but I felt a new fear. A fear spilling from my ghosts. A fear of me.

"Let's get inside," Jake said, forcing me to turn around.

Mrs. Hearth was standing at the curb, hand to her breast and gasping. When I met her eyes, which were glowing a faint yellow, she heaved a sigh and stepped forward, resting her hand on my other shoulder. At the very moment she touched me, I could feel her magic start to calm me down.

Steps sounded on the asphalt behind me, and when I glanced over my shoulder, Catherina had run to Connor's side, but she wasn't helping him up. She was staring open-mouthed after us. She was so, so pale. Like she'd seen a ghost. The thought made me giggle. Cornelia was still crying as hard as she could.

Then I was forced up the stairs and inside, and the door slammed and locked behind me.

12

"What did you do out there?" Jake hissed. "And where did that come from?" He was pointing at the owl on my shoulder, currently grooming my hair with its beak, which kind of hurt and kind of didn't.

"You can see it?" I asked.

"We all...can," Mrs. Hearth answered from the seat by the wall. She'd slumped down the moment we were through the door.

Her eyes had stopped glowing the yellow of magic, but she was still gasping for breath and clutching at her chest. Abigail was sitting by her side, one hand resting on her mother's leg, the other gripped so hard around a crystal it had turned white. Sara was standing in the opening leading into the living room, staring at all of us in turn. My ghosts were moving as well. Elizabeth had grabbed hold of the three youngest ghosts and was pulling them away from me, their fear clear on their faces and thrumming through the chords between us. I felt the same fear from Eleanor and aunt Ellie, but also anger. The two of them were talking, trying to be louder than the other as Magdalena cried, and Elizabeth shushed her. All the sounds were giving me a headache, but at the realization that everyone could see my owl, the ghosts stopped talking, but they were still angry and confused.

And there was so much confusion. Not just from my ghosts and the living people around me, but it was moving along other threads connected to that spot within my chest. The feelings running along those threads were weaker, and I didn't know anything about the owner of the feelings like I did with my gaggle, but I knew that every thread was connected to another ghost, another spirit. How I knew, I had no idea.

"What happened?" Sara finally asked. "Is grams ok?"

"Get me my amethyst," Abigail said, not looking away from her mother. Sara didn't even nod before she started running toward the stairs.

"What's going on?" I asked, taking a step toward Mrs. Hearth, but Jake and aunt Ellie stepped in my way. Even Eleanor made sure to stand behind them.

"Come with me," Jake said and grabbed my arm. The owl turned its head toward him and partly spread its wings, as if ready to attack again, but even before I'd finished the thought of it calming down it returned to grooming my hair.

I let Jake lead me into the kitchen, where he placed me in one of the chairs. When I sat, the owl jumped to my lap as I started removing my winter clothing, putting them over the back of one of the other chairs. On the floors above us, I could hear Sara sprint around before she flew down the stairs again. Jake closed the door to the kitchen so I didn't get a chance to see her zoom past. Eleanor and aunt Ellie had followed right through the wall and were now flanking the door like two guards. Eleanor was crying silently.

There was so much crying these days.

Someone was knocking at the front door, and in the partial silence of the house, I heard it open and Sara's angry voice before it slammed shut again. I could picture Connor standing there, ready to knock again, but he seemed to think better of it. I couldn't deal with him right now anyway.

Hands on the table, I was picking away at the polish covering my nails at an alarming rate, following Jake with my eyes.

Finally, after roaming the kitchen a few times, Jake sat down opposite me. He'd removed his outwear as well, but goosebumps covered his skin.

"What did you do out there?" he asked, looking me square in the eye.

"I'd like to know the same," aunt Ellie said.

"What do you mean?" I answered, turning toward the two ghosts.

"Hey!" Jake said, reaching over the table to grab me.

The owl, who had been grooming itself in my lap, lifted its head and opened its beak and wings. I lowered a hand and stroked its head, not taking my eyes off aunt Ellie. "Just a moment, Jake. Aunt Ellie?"

Fear was tingling in my chest and I wasn't sure if it was theirs or mine.

Aunt Ellie gave a sigh. "I mean, how did you do that?"

"Do what?"

"Control us like that?"

"Control you?"

"Wait," Jake said, leaning heavily on the table but not reaching for me. The owl was still glaring at him. "You controlled the ghosts?"

"*Oui*, you did," Eleanor said, her accent so thick I hardly would have understood her if not for the link between us. "Your anger became ours, and your wish to hurt him. It filled us up, and despite us not wanting too, we could not help ourselves.

We were hurting him."

"I..." I turned to aunt Ellie, who only nodded. "I made you hurt him?"

"Not only him," Jake said. "The air around you was freezing cold, but not a normal cold. 'tis was the cold of a nightmare. The kind that sits deep in your bones for hours after you wake, following you in the shadows. The air around you was the pure cold of terror."

"But how is that possible?" I asked and turned to the ghosts. "How could I do that to you?"

Jake turned pale as I spoke, and he was shivering as he leaned away from me. "You're a necromancer," he said in a whisper.

I snapped around to look at him. "No, I'm not. Mrs. Hearth said I was a shaman. You said I was a shaman."

"Which explains the owl and how you can see the deeper planes, but not how you control spirits. Only necromancers can control spirits, and necromancers don't exist."

"Then why are you calling me one?" I was wrapping my arms around myself, feeling all those threads connected to me. The owl, as if sensing my confusion and fear, pushed as close to me as it could. Its heartbeat in tandem with mine.

"Because they were real once," Jake said as he stood and started to pace again. "There was a cult of them many genera-tions ago. Witches with the Sight that did something, a kind of ritual, to take control of the spirits. If they survived the ritual, they could summon and control whole armies of the dead. Some of the strongest could even put spirits back into dead bodies or summon the spirits from beyond the Veil."

"Wait, I don't understand."

"Neither do we. These witches, they turned bad. They were hunted and killed, and to this day a witch born with the Sight may find herself shunned."

"But there are no necromancers anymore?"

Jake stopped in his pacing and turned to me. "Not before now, no."

"How do you know that's what happened? I haven't been through any ritual. I wasn't really able to see ghosts before I died myself, and then only those that were killed by the same curse as me," I was gesticulating toward the ghosts by the door, even if he couldn't see them, hugging the owl close to my chest with the other hand. "I haven't seen any other ghosts."

"No, but you see the ghosts of memories. That's why you couldn't stay at your house yesterday, wasn't it? And you feel the ghost of emotions like you did in the yard. That is a shaman power. Maybe you've been able to do it all the time, but haven't known about it, and something that happened recently made you –" He cut himself off and slumped back into his chair, biting at his lower lip as his eyes flicked back and forth. It looked like he was reading.

"What?" I asked. What was going on? Was this my fault as well?

Before I had the chance to reach forward and touch him, the door opened and Sara stepped in. The rings around her eyes looked almost black against her pale skin. She looked drained. In her hands, she carried a thin silver chain with a multitude of jagged purple crystals on it, ending in a clear quartz.

I stood so fast the owl tumbled to the floor with a squawk.

Sara stopped just inside the door and looked at the owl that was basking its wings to right itself before she looked at my hands, nervously chipping away at my nail polish. Her eyes jumped to Jake.

"Oh," was all she said before she moved toward the counter.

"He's reading."

"What?" I asked, turning with her.

"He told you 'bout his memory thing?" I nodded. "He's reading 'bout something. Any idea what?" As she talked, she put the chain carefully in a shining silver bowl in the windowsill before she bent and started rooting through one of the bottom cupboards.

"How is Mrs. Hearth?" I asked instead of answering. I sat back down, but the owl didn't seem to trust my lap and flew up to sit on the chair that held my clothes. I had no idea how to hide it back into myself, and then I thought of the mark that had been on my chest after it emerged the first time.

"Grams's gonna be fine. She was exhausted after dealing with all those feelings you sent out. She just needs to be balanc... what're you doing?" She was holding a hemp bag of something against her stomach and looking at me as I was unbuttoning my shirt and trying to see my chest. There was just the faintest shadow left of what had seemed like a tattoo before the owl emerged, but it was still there.

"Just checking something," I said, hurriedly buttoning up my shirt again. "So she's fine?"

Sara narrowed her eyes at me before shrugging and turned to pour salt into the silver bowl. "Yeah, but she needs to rest."

"Can you tell her I'm sorry?"

"Tell her yourself at dinner. She'll be fine by then." Her hands were shaking as she put away the bag of salt, so I wasn't sure I believed her.

"What are you doing?" I asked, hoping to fill the heavy silence between us. I could still hear Magdalena crying, and aunt Ellie and Eleanor may have moved out of the room but I could still hear them talking just outside the door.

"Cleansing mom's amethyst chain. She usually doesn't like others touching her crystals, but she needs to be with grams a little longer."

"Crystals?"

Sara waved it away and slumped into one of the empty chairs, putting her face in her hands. "Later."

"Sorry."

"Don't worry 'bout it."

"Not about this, about everything. All of this is my fault."

She split two of her fingers apart so she could look at me with one eye. "Why do you say that?"

"All those feelings out there that she was dealing with? I think they came from me and were amplified through my ghosts. I was... doing something to them and it wasn't good. Jake thinks I might be a necromancer, but I have no idea what that means and I'm scared because the ghosts are scared of me and angry at me and I don't know what to do about this stupid owl!" My voice had risen while I talked until I was almost shouting. Sara lowered her hands and stared at me, wide-eyed and open-mouthed. "And Connor's back and I have no idea how to deal with him. Not after everything he left me to do on my own." My high tone died to a low growl and I stared at my hands, not able to look at the fear in Sara's eyes anymore.

I'd made her afraid of me as well.

We sat in silence, listening to the house move and settle around us. Somewhere above, Mrs. Hearth and Abigail were in the same room, hopefully resting. I could feel the ghosts but not hear them. At least they were calming down. The owl had stopped moving and was just sitting on its chair, eyes closed but opening every time one of us moved. It would look groggily at us, then shake itself and go back to sleep.

The silence stretched until Jake's eyes stopped moving and he yawned. The sudden sound and movement snapped the bubble around us and Sara finally looked at me. The fear was gone from her eyes but her brow was still knit and her lips pressed together.

Jake blinked at his girlfriend before reaching out a hand to take hers. "What did she tell you?" He asked her, clearly reading her face as well as I did.

"Not much, just that you think she's a..." she couldn't say the word, and ended up closing her mouth and shaking her head.

"Yeah, I think I might be wrong about that," Jake said, turning to me. Sara closed her eyes at his words. "But I don't know what you are, either," he continued. "We witches have our stories of necromancers. The darkest of dark witches. Shamans have the stories of the ghost-witch."

"A ghost-witch?" I asked, glancing toward the wall that was hiding my ghosts from view.

Jake shook his head as if reading my thoughts. "You're ability to see and talk to ghosts isn't because of that. That's a natural shamanic power, as far as we can tell. But your ability to control them, might be because of it. Shamans hold their stories close, and few chroniclers have been able to learn much more than what is common knowledge today."

"Then why bring it up?" Sara asked.

"Because a ghost-witch is a shaman that has risen from the dead with murder in its heart. The only problem is that the shaman had to perform black magic before it died, and there are signs you can look for. Lizzie don't have them. To top it off, the ghost-witch doesn't seem to have anything to do with ghosts other than being one herself." Sara and I looked at each other. "But I'm bringing it up because I don't know if a shaman can become a necromancer, or if a witch can become a ghost-witch, and neither did any of my line." He looked angry as he said this, like he was taking the lack of knowledge as a personal offense.

"So, we don't know nothing?" Sara asked.

"Both yes and no." When he didn't continue, Sara squeezed his hand hard and he grimaced in pain. "Fine! Fine. I think the creature we're looking for is a wendigo."

"A what-igo?" I asked.

Jake let Sara go and lifted a finger, then he stood and jogged out of the kitchen.

"He does that," Sara said, scowling after her boyfriend.

"He seems really nice," I said. "But I never thought you'd settle for a bookworm."

She snorted. "Neither did I, but he's good for me."

"Good."

We looked at each other, no fear or any hard feelings between us. Just relief and joy, it seemed like.

Jake returned with a big book in his hands.

"Seriously," Sara murmured and rolled her eyes. "He lugs those books everywhere he goes. Why would he even need some old tome at my childhood crush's mom's funeral anyway?"

Jake glared at her. "Just for situations like this."

"And how often does that happen?"

He glared even harder before turning his eyes to me. "This," he said, laying the leather-bound book on the table and starting to leaf through it. "'tis all we know of indigenous lore. One of my mentors traveled a lot and talked to a lot of storytellers, even shamans," he grinned at me. "And while they wouldn't tell him about their magic, they did share their peoples' stories."

"Doesn't he have this book in his head already? Why bring

it?" I asked Sara as Jake continued leafing through the book.

She shrugged. "Yes, but if he haven't read in a while, it'll take a lot to dredge up the memories. Ironically, he brought this and two others along as some ''light reading'' for this trip." She rolled her eyes and scowled at her boyfriend in a way so warm it made my heart ache.

Jake stopped at a page and turned the book toward me. "Does that look familiar?"

The pages were yellowed and brittle with age, and I couldn't help wondering what it was worth and at the same time cringe at how Jake treated the old tome. All the writing was done by hand, snaking its way across the page. On the page next to it was a drawing, and I couldn't help myself leaning forward and touching it.

The creature was long and lean, too thin and tall to really be human. According to the notes at the bottom of the page, it was expected to stand over two meters tall if it stood full height, but the wendigo was drawn crouched like an animal on all fours. Its hands were thin and clawed, with only four fingers on each and with an extra joint. Its body was covered in black, coarse fur, only pulling back at the fingers and toes and head, which was shaped like a wolf's skull with antlers. The description at the bottom stated that while the head was always a clean skull, it was individual to each wendigo if there were more skeletal parts on the body. Some had been known to have open rib cages at the chest with fur growing between the bones, while others had bones and sinew on their hands and feet, or the spine pushing through the skin.

"Lizzie?" Sara asked, and I pulled back from the book, having actually stood from my chair to have a closer look.

"Yes," I said, biting at one of my nails. "Yes, that looks right."

12

"I thought wendigos were cannibalistic people?" Sara asked. "Least that's what they talked 'bout on that *Sleepy Hollow* show. Or scorned lovers, like on *Charmed.*"

Jake shook his head and closed the book. His brow was furrowed and he was chewing on his bottom lip again, his eyes jumping between the two of us and the owl, its wings ruffled.

"Both yes and no," he said again, seeming to force himself to sit down instead of pacing, the book hugged to his chest. "'tis what we want humanity to believe. Wendigos are spirits, locked away with all the others. When strong enough, they can possess humans. The wendigos are always hungry, and they want meat. Their own bodies aren't of our plane, so they try to steal energy from spirits and the world until they are strong enough to affect our plane, then they try to oppress someone and go on a killing spree."

"Oppress?" I asked.

"Subdue the soul and take over the body," Sara answered.

I looked between the witch and the chronicler. "But if they're really supposed to be locked away, why is there one here now?"

Jake's eyes gleamed and he leaned across the table. "That's the interesting thing! Remember I mentioned the Veil earlier?" I nodded. "Right, so the Veil is –"

"Not something we're gonna discuss now," Sara said, voice as stern as her grandmother's as she stopped Jake's hands from gesticulating across the table, the book forgotten in his lap. "You've stifled seven yawns since coming out of your memories, and it always drains you when going far back as you did now."

"I did not –" Jake began, but a look from Sara made him shut his mouth.

"I know how long it takes you to do your reading. You went back to the beginning, and so you should be exhausted." She turned to me. "And you're tired too. Don't argue. I know your tells as well, remember?" I blushed and looked at my hands. "So you will both go to your respective rooms, not talk anymore about wendigos or the Veil or spirits or anything. Jake, you will sleep. Lizzie, I would ask you to sleep as well, but I don't think grams can help you right now, so it would be at your own risk."

"That's fine. I don't want sleep anyway," I answered.

"What'll you do?"

I opened my mouth to answer but was cut off as my phone rang for what seemed like the hundredth time. I'd hoped it would stop on its own, but was sick of waiting and hoping. Lifting a finger, I found my phone with the other hand and turned off both sound and vibrate, not even looking to see the caller-ID.

"There," I said and put the phone away, meeting Sara's eyes. "I can't rest now. Not knowing there's a creature out there hunting my gaggle of ghosts."

"Fright of ghosts," Jake said.

We both turned to look at him.

"What?" Sara asked.

"A group of ghosts is called a fright of ghosts, not a gaggle."

"Ok," I said, drawing out the word. "Anyway. I can't rest now that I know something is actively hunting them. They're my responsibility, whatever they're called, and it's my fault one of them is gone." Sara opened her mouth to say something, probably to comfort me, but I shook my head. "It is. If I hadn't been so selfish, I would have helped them move on the moment I was better. But I didn't. I wallowed in my own sorrow and misery, and now one of them is dead." My voice turned hard and angry. It was either that, or I started to sob again, and there'd been more than enough crying for a lifetime.

"So how will you help them? We don't know anyone that knows anything about shamans," Jake said after another yawn.

"My powers must come from somewhere, right? If I can find my grandparents, I should find another shaman."

"How'll you do that?" Sara asked.

"Start at the beginning."

"And where's that?"

I turned to look at aunt Ellie. She was standing by the wall, arms crossed and not looking at me.

"Loyde House," I said, the words sending a ripple of mixed emotions through the thread between us. "Where mom was raised."

13

Jake immediately started pushing about how I was going to figure it out and saying that he could help, but Sara would have none of it.

"You, you stupid chronicler, are going to bed. I'll help Lizzie," she said, pushing both of us out of the kitchen.

"Actually," I said, and Sara scowled at me. "I need to do this myself. I know where to start. I just need mom's little black book."

"Black book?" Jake asked as Sara made a face.

"She gave it to Mrs. Hearth when she got diagnosed," I said, not looking at anyone, living or dead. "Sara, could you please ask your grams where it is?"

Her glare felt heavy, but it lightened when she rolled her eyes. "Fine! I'll talk to grams if you can get this idiot to bed?" She pushed Jake as she said it.

"Aye, aye, captain," I answered, saluting.

Sara rolled her eyes and jogged past us and toward the stairs.

"You don't have to do what she tells you to, you know," Jake said conspiratorially.

I laughed. It was a little forced, but somewhere deep down, it was true as well. "Oh, yes, I do! I'm not risking getting on her bad side."

Jake smiled. It didn't reach his eyes, but just like my laugh, part of it was true. "So you've been there as well, have you?" I nodded, and his grin grew a little wider.

We walked up the stairs in comfortable silence. I had never been this relaxed around new people before, and I couldn't help but wonder if it was Mrs. Hearth's calming magic working on me, or if it was just the way Jake was. Or the fact that Sara had chosen him for some reason, and I would trust Sara with my life. If she trusted him, I trusted him. Any friend of her's, and all that.

Sara was standing at the first-floor landing, waiting for us, arms crossed and foot tapping.

"I think I'm in trouble," Jake stage whispered.

I bumped his shoulder with mine. "Hurry, and I'll distract her."

He winked and jumped a step to give Sara a quick kiss on the cheek before he ran toward the bathroom. Sara turned after him, opening her mouth to say something, but I was before her in a second.

"Is that it?" I asked, pointing to the little book in her hands.

Sighing, she nodded and marched through the bedroom door to dump the book on the desk there. "I'll be back when I've dealt with him," she said, pointing toward the bathroom where Jake was currently locked away. "I swear, the two of you together'll be the death of me."

"You love us," I said.

She grinned and patted my ass as we passed each other. I let out a surprised yelp and turned, clutching my behind in both hands as Sara's grin widened.

"Indeed, I do," she answered and turned her back, swagging her own hips a little.

Eyes glued to her, I managed to close the door and lean against it. Letting out a deep sigh, I listened to Sara and Jake talk as they made their way to Emma's room. The owl jumped from my hands and flew to the bed, where it started grooming itself again.

A yawn forced its way out of me, but even as I glanced at the bed, I knew I didn't dare sleep. Not without Sara or Mrs. Hearth here to protect me. Closing my eyes, I dragged my hands through my hair. I couldn't rely on them forever. There had to be another way to keep the dreams at bay. At the thought, something tickled at the back of my mind, but I was too mentally exhausted from all the feelings of the morning to grip the thought properly. It didn't help that I hadn't eaten anything since yesterday. I'd gone longer without proper food in times of stress, but I knew it addled my mind. Not to mention I was hungry, but I couldn't think of what I might want to eat.

Letting another yawn go, I opened my eyes and pushed away from the door. I couldn't sleep anyway. There was too much going on, and I had work to do.

"So," I began, turning to the owl. "How do I get you back inside me?"

As if understanding, it fluffed its feathers and spread its wings. On an instinct that wasn't mine, I lifted my arm just as the owl pushed from its perch. It landed on my arm, claws cutting into my naked skin. I winced and the owl cocked its head.

"Guess I should wear long sleeves from now on," I murmured. "Do you know how to get back inside me?"

The owl blinked its green-blue eyes, the same as mine, before leaning forward. Its forehead touched the area between my breasts, where the shadow of its head was barely visible. I could feel the warmth of it seeping into the hollow, and I opened myself to it. The shape of the owl dissolved into a thin, white mist and was gone. Or, not completely. I could feel it settling in to sleep inside me, filling the empty space and me with a warmth and completeness I wasn't aware I'd lacked before this very moment.

"Well, ok then," I said to no-one.

There was still so much to learn, but my body and mind seemed to know how to do some of it. It was fascinating and scary all at the same time.

Secondly, I needed to apologize to my ghosts. I hoped they knew I didn't do what I did on purpose, that I didn't even know I could do it until they told me, but that did not mean it was ok and that I shouldn't respect how it made them feel. They were, after all, still human.

As if sensing me thinking of them, aunt Ellie walked through the door. I turned toward her, an uncertain smile on my face.

"You wanted to talk?" she asked, weariness in her voice.

"To all of you, if that's possible?"

She only nodded before disappearing again.

I stood there, in the middle of a room that wasn't mine, and waited for what felt like forever but was only seconds until the gaggle, fright, all filled the little room. Eleanor sat on the bed, her legs swollen from her pregnancy. Magdalena curled up beside her, face hidden against the woman's breast and looking at me through the corner of her eye. Elizabeth held the twins close, trying to look adult with her chin high and back straight, but the way she hugged her siblings betrayed her uncertainty. Aunt Ellie stood in the middle of the room, arms crossed and looking straight at me.

"I want to apologize," I began. "I know that isn't enough,

that what I did to you was inhumane. You deserve better, and I'm really sorry I did that. I didn't know I could, but that doesn't make it ok. I should have realized what I was doing the moment it happened and stopped it." Aunt Ellie's tight face loosened a little as I spoke. "And I'm really sorry I have neglected you. I never thought anything could happen to you, and so I put off looking for a way to help you move on as I dealt with my own grief. I was really selfish, and it has put you all in danger. I still don't know how to help you move on, but I will do my best to find out and get you out of harm's way as fast as I can."

As I spoke, aunt Ellie stepped forward until she was standing right in front of me. She couldn't touch me, but when she rested her hand just over my cheek, I could almost feel the warmth of it. "We appreciate and accept your apology, and we forgive you for everything. Just don't do it again."

I shook my head so hard it gave me a headache. "I won't."

"Good." Aunt Ellie stepped back and glanced at the other ghosts, who all nodded.

I let out a sigh of relief.

"So what are you going to do with the others?" Elizabeth asked.

It took me a moment to realize she was talking about the other ghosts. Those I'd summoned and could feel drawing ever closer. Those extra threads connected to that cold spot inside of me that I didn't have a name for. They were other ghosts, spirits, that I had bound to me.

"I honestly don't know. I have to help them move on as well, I guess. The only way I can do that is to figure out how, and for that, I need help."

I lifted the book Sara had found for me and waved it around a little.

Aunt Ellie, jaw still clenched, nodded.

14

Slumping down on the bed, I stared at the book for a second. This book had followed mom since she was a teen. It held so many of her secrets. It felt a little weird to open it, but I knew I needed it. Not for me, but for the ghosts. This was their only chance.

I opened the book to the first page. Mom's serious handwriting beamed at me in fading ink, and I had to smile when I saw it, remembering that mom had two handwritings. A serious one she used when signing documents or writing important notes, and the normal one that she used to everyday things. It was more playful, somehow, while the serious was was, well, serious.

This book contains:
- *Personal information*
- *Bank accounts and savings*
- *Internet accounts*
- *Email*
- *Important people with emails and phone numbers*

At the bottom of the page, in ink much fresher and a different color, stood:

– Location of last will and testament, and other important papers

She must have written it after she got diagnosed.

Hurriedly looking away, I focused on the first point of her list and started leafing through the book.

Mom's personal information was placed neatly across the pages. There were her full name and the house where she was raised, as well as the name and number of the housefathers. She'd also updated numbers and emails to the kids she'd been raised with. If nothing else, I could ask them for help.

Using my cell phone, I typed in the number for Loyde House. A weird feeling of trepidation and expectation slithered through my stomach as I waited for someone to pick up. Mom never talked much about the place she grew up. She'd once told me she'd been really lucky, staying at Loyde House, and that she thought the housefathers had saved her life by taking her in. I'd looked the place up once, and it seemed to be a farm/orphanage. It seemed like a nice place.

The sound of a baby crying exploded through the phone, and I almost dropped it. It wasn't just whimpering, but screaming, then the sound grew muffled.

"Loyde House, you're talking to Micah Loyde?"

For one second, I didn't know what to answer. I still didn't want people to call me Lizzie, it felt wrong in so many ways, but I still hadn't found a replacement. "Yeah, hi. Uhm, my name is Lizzie Key, and I'm the daughter of Nancy Key, maiden name Doe, that grew up with you?"

Almost before my words were out, I heard a sound on the other end of the line. Like someone pulling in an uneven breath. "Yes. We were at your mother's funeral. I'm so sorry for your loss."

"Oh, thanks."

"So how may I help you, Lizzie Key?"

"I was actually wondering about my mother. If she was looking for her parents or ever found any other relatives? Do you know anything about that?"

Micah smacked his lips a few times before answering. "Not that I can think off right now, but I have her file in the office." He hesitated. "I do not feel all that comfortable talking about this over the phone. Do you think you could come visit?" When I didn't answer immediately, he went on. "You see, we've just got a new member to our household a few days back, and Eli and I already went away to go to your mother's funeral. The only reason we could leave yesterday was because Alice had a home project and could watch Tommy."

I blinked against the barage of words and names. "Yes, sure. When can I come?"

"I'm home with Tommy all day. The other kids and Eli will show up around dinner-time."

I nodded once before I realized that he couldn't see me. "Yes. I can come today if that's ok? It's an hour to drive, so I could be there around lunch?"

"That would be great. I've always hated cooking just for myself."

"No, I didn't mean –"

He spoke over me. "Will you be bringing anyone?"

"Uh, maybe."

"Great! I'll whip something up that can hold in case there's some traffic or such. I'll find those files as well so you don't have to wait for me to get them when you're here. I'm looking forward to meeting you under better circumstances, Lizzie."

"You too," I answered, having forgotten his name between

all the other names he'd mentioned.

After we hung up, I sat staring at my phone for a little while. What did I expect to find out there? A file with mom's personal information was probably all they had. But, if nothing else, getting to see the place where mom was raised could be interesting. I knew she'd kept in touch with some of the people from her upbringing, but I'd never met any of them except at the funeral, and that didn't really count. I hardly remembered the event, not to mention strangers that might or might not have been there.

Dragging my pinky from my lips to stop chewing on the nail, I stood and headed for the kitchen.

Sara stood at the bottom of the stairs, a tray in her hands. On it was a glass of orange juice and the bottom of a homemade bun with butter and cheese on top.

"What's up?" she asked as she stepped in my way.

"I got a hold of Loyde House and have an appointment," I said and tried to step past her, but she made sure to block me with the tray.

"When?"

"Now."

"Ok, then." Sara supported the tray with one hand and lifted the glass. "Drink."

"Sara –"

"Drink! You're not going nowhere without something in you."

I scowled but grabbed the glass and downed the content. It was sour and cold and cleared my mind better than any coffee or tea could. Still scowling, I set the glass upside down on the tray.

"Good, now the bun."

"I'm not hungry." I was. My stomach felt hollow, but just the thought of eating gave me a bellyache.

"If you don't eat, you'll get us into an accident."

"Us?"

She tossed her head to flip her green bangs out of her eyes. "Yeah, I'm coming."

"No, you're not."

"Yeah, I am, especially if you won't eat."

I grabbed the bun and took a bite. Something moved in my stomach, but I wasn't sure if it was hunger or nauseusness. I swallowed the bite and my stomach grumbled in dissatisfaction. It didn't want cheese. It wanted meat. The thought made my mouth water and I took another bite to stop the pictures of a rare steak in my head from getting hold. Even as I chewed the cheese and dough, part of me craved the bloody meat, and it made me a little sick.

"Ok, then," Sara said, grinning. "I'm still coming."

"Why?" I mumbled around the food in my mouth, too preoccupied to argue anymore.

"'cause four ears are better than two. I'll get the keys."

She hurried toward the kitchen, humming to herself and swinging her behind in a way that she knew drew my gaze. As she stepped through the door, she gave me a wink that made me blush.

15

I got dressed and left the house, Sara's bustling about the kitchen still in my ears, and forced down another bite of the bun to please her.

Something white moved against the dark grey sky, and I looked up. It was a bird. Hope surged in my chest for half a heartbeat before I realized it wasn't a crow. The bird landed on the stone pillar marking Mr. Galvin's driveway and turned its head so it could look at me with one, beady black eye. The eye shone in the street light.

"That is a good sign," Elizabeth said beside me and I jumped at her sudden appearance.

"What is?" I asked, not taking my eyes off the bird.

"The dove. A white dove is the soul of Christ our savior."

A dove, that was what it was. I hadn't been able to see from this distance, only see that it wasn't the crow that had saved me, us, in the Grey World.

"Shouldn't it be somewhere South enjoying the sun?" I asked absentmindedly, trying to shake the memories of the night mom died. Of the crack as the Red Woman broke her neck.

"Who should be enjoying the sun?" Sara asked as she exited the door and skipped down the porch steps, holding a steaming travel mug in one hand.

"That dove," I said, pointing to it.

The bird jerked at my movement but stayed put.

Sara stopped by my side and looked at it for a moment. "Yeah, it should."

"Why do you think it's here?"

"Who knows, maybe it's too sick to fly?"

"I saw it fly just now. Do you know of any supernatural doves? Like weredoves or something?"

Sara snorted, and Elizabeth gasped, staring at me like I'd grown an extra head.

"No, can't say I do. Maybe Jake does? We'll ask when we get back. Want me to drive?"

"Sure, thanks," I tossed the keys to her and moved toward the passenger door, Elizabeth following hot on my heels. I could feel her displeasure as we moved.

"It was just a question. As Jake said, I don't know anything," I muttered. This seemed to mollify her a little. "So, will you all be coming or just you?"

"All of us," Eleanor answered from the stoop where she was waddling her way down the steps with Magdalena balanced on one hip and the twins running around her. Aunt Ellie was right behind her, arms lifted a little, as if ready to catch her should she fall or the twins trip her.

"I don't think you can all fit," I said, staring at the small car.

"Can we sit on the roof?!" Jonathan asked, sprinting toward me and starting to climb the hood before any of us adults had a chance to answer. When we did, however, it was a solid no.

Jonathan slid off the hood with a pout that would make any six-year-old brat envious.

Inside the car, Sara leaned over the seat and opened the passenger door. "Coming?"

"Yes, just a matter of logistics."

"What?"

"All my ghosts want to come, but we can't fit them all into the car."

"Can't some of 'em ride on the roof?" The twins whooped with joy as Eleanor, Elizabeth, and I shot Sara a dark look. She only saw mine, but it appeared to be enough. "What?"

I sighed. "Fine, guess you can ride on the roof, that should make room for the rest of you..."

My sentence trailed off as I opened the back door and Elizabeth crawled in first, taking Magdalena from Eleanor's arms. Eleanor muttered something about carriages being so small these days as she pressed her pregnant self into the seat behind mine. Aunt Ellie walked around and right through the door to sit behind Sara.

Closing the door, I climbed inside to my own seat as the twins scrambled up the hood and front window to sit on the roof.

In the back seat, Elizabeth stood and pushed her head through the ceiling. Her voice was muffled but clear enough: "If you get cold, come inside. You should not get a chill."

"We can't get chills," Johana answered.

Elizabeth's voice was stern when she answered, but I tuned her out and smiled tiredly at Sara. "Let's just drive."

She looked at me with raised eyebrows for a moment before she nodded and started the car.

"So, what's the story with Jake?" I asked as Sara pulled out of McKey-street and onto the main road through Sky Harbour.

"What story?" she asked.

"He told me the two of you found each other when you needed it the most; how did that happen?"

"Coincidence?"

"Uhu. Come on, spill! It's been so long, and I want to know what your life looks like now."

She finally looked at me. Just a glance before returning to the road, but it was there. I poked her in the shoulder and she sighed but I saw the twitch in her cheek: She wanted to smile.

"Come on!" I pleaded, making my voice whiny.

"Fine!" She hit my hand away when I moved to poke her again. "What you wanna know?"

I leaned back in my seat, my thoughts for a second drowned out by the arguing of the ghosts in the back. I noticed aunt Ellie's voice wasn't among them and turned to look. She was staring out the window, lost in her own thoughts.

"Lizzie?" Sara asked, poking me this time, on the nose.

"Yeah, sorry. How you met. He's a chronicler, right? How did a chronicler and a witch get together?"

"I looked him up."

"What?" I pictured Sara standing on his doorstep, flowers in hand, and proclaiming they should be together the moment he opened the door.

Sara laughed. "Nothing like what you're thinking."

"How do you know what I'm thinking?"

"I know you. No, I looked him up to ask 'bout my powers."

"Why? And what are your powers, anyway?"

"What do you wanna know? 'bout my powers or 'bout Jake and me?"

"Both?"

"One at a time."

"Fine, stick with you and Jake for now."

She chuckled. "I looked him up to ask 'bout my powers because mom kept nagging me 'bout binding them." I wanted to ask what she meant by that but kept my mouth closed. Sara noticed and shot me a smile before she continued. "So we met in Dartmouth and had a cup of coffee. This was a few years ago."

"When?"

"I'm telling a story here!"

"Sorry! But when? Were we still together?"

She shook her head. "No, we weren't. So I looked him up and we met in Dartmouth and took a cup of coffee, or hot chocolate for me as I didn't drink coffee back then, and we talked, and we got on well. We've a lot of history in common and knowing you're not alone is such a relief. So the drink became lunch, then dinner, then I had to go. I didn't think we'd stay in touch, but when I got home, he'd sent me an email. He became the person I turned to when I couldn't turn to you. My harbor in a storm, as Emma called it." I leaned back in my seat, unable to look at her. I'd never known why we broke up, never understood

Sara's need for distance, and now I wanted to ask. Maybe it had something to do with her being a witch? With her powers? I shook my head, trying to dislodge the small sliver of hope moving in the back of my mind. Now that I knew she was a witch, could we work out? But no way was I getting between Jake and Sara. They were too good for each other. "So, when I turned eighteen, mom kicked me out. We were in a rough place then, and I think she was afraid of me. She gave me an ultimatum. Either I find a new place to live, or I bind my magic. I moved out. Joke's on her, for I'm still part of the coven, so blah," she stuck her tongue out at nothing. "But I had nowhere to go, and somehow I ended up on Jake's stoop. He let me stay there a while for free, then I got a job and started paying rent, then one thing led to another, and here we are."

A silence fell over the car. I wasn't sure if I should be looking at her or out the window.

"Ok," I finally said. "So what's your power?"

Sara drew a deep breath. "It's luck."

I snorted. "Luck? How does that work?"

Sara still wasn't looking at me. "I take luck from the world around me," she said. "I have an aura that's active all the time if I don't turn it off. That's why when I sleep close to you and you wish to not dream 'bout the wendigo, you don't. My aura increases the chance of you getting what you wish for. Get it?"

"A little, I think. Why turn it off, though? Having luck like that..." I stopped for a moment, thinking back to school. "Was that how you made the teacher never question you in class, and when they did they only asked questions you knew the answers to?"

Sara smiled a small smile that didn't reach her eyes. "Yeah. You've no idea how chewed out I got for that one."

16

"But why?"

"Luck can corrupt people. I can't control what kind of luck my power gives me, but it would always try to give me what I want, no matter where it takes it from. Like if I'm at a job interview and I turn on my aura while alone in the room with the interviewer, it will steal some of the luck from the people outside, making them stumble over their words when it's their turn, and making me not. If I'm in a fight, I might use some of the luck to avoid getting punched or hit, but if I wanna hurt the person I'm fighting, I'll be able to hit just right to hurt 'em, maybe even kill 'em."

She grew quiet again and I sat back, remembering school. We hadn't gone to the same Middle School or Kindergarten, but everyone in Sky Harbour went to the same Junior High. Because we knew each other from before, Sara and I started hanging out, and soon we did more than that. Sky Harbour being a small town, the other kids started picking on us when they saw us kissing behind the school one day. Sara got into a lot of fights because of it. She never got hit, but somehow always managed to beat her opponents without hurting them too much.

It wasn't until the summer before High School started that she really hurt someone.

We'd been together for two years and Emma's boyfriend's brother was back in town. We were at a party at his place, invited by Emma. Sara and I were dancing when the brother came up and tried to split us up. Talking about how girls like us just needed to get some dick to know what was good for us. Later that night, he followed me to the bathroom and tried to make good on his promise. Sara heard me scream and came to help me. The guy ended up in a coma from hitting his head on the sink. The Hearths visited him at the hospital a lot, and he came out of it a few months later, but things deteriorated between Sara and me after that, and it was almost a blessing when we broke up.

"That's what really happened that night, wasn't it?" I asked now. Sara knew what I was talking about and nodded. "And why you visited him in the hospital so many times. You guy's used your powers to try and save him." Sara nodded again. "Sara, I'm so sorry. That was my fault, I..." My words trailed off. I had no idea what to say. If I could even make it better. But it wasn't her fault.

"It was not your fault he tried to rape you," Sara said, voice hard. I glanced at her, seeing her set jaw and her knuckles white against the wheel.

Noticing my look, she drew a deep breath and forced her shoulders to relax a little. "So that's why I don't use my powers actively," she said. "If I let it run wild, I may end up hurting people, and if I stop caring 'bout that, I may turn dark. Luck can corrupt its user. Witch lore is full of women getting addicted to luck and turning to dark magic. I won't let that happen to me, so I don't use it unless I have to."

"So, you've used it a lot more than usual because of me?" I asked.

Finally, she looked at me. "No. I can't concentrate on keeping it down when I sleep, so it'll be active then anyway."

I nodded, remembering Mrs. Hearth saying something of the sort.

A heavy silence fell between us; both of us lost in our own thoughts and memories. At least I thought so, until Sara spoke again, her voice forcefully happy.

"You can say something now."

What to say? I wanted to ask more about her powers, but it

was clear it wasn't something she wanted to talk about, that it hurt her. "Abigail really did that? Gave you that ultimatum, I mean?" Yeah, that's a lot safer.

She sighed. "There's a lot 'bout our family you don't know."

"Maybe that will change now," I said before I had time to think about it.

Sara glanced at me before she let go of the wheel with one hand and took mine. She squeezed, and I squeezed back.

"So, what 'bout your life? This Mark guy, what's up with that?"

My light mood fell away and I scowled at the car in front of us. We were on the freeway now, and Sara drove past it when she noticed my glare.

"What did that car ever do to you?" she asked as we pulled in in front of it.

I couldn't help chuckling.

I told her in short strokes how Mark and I met at a mutual friend's party where I had a little too much to drink because of what was going on with mom, and woke up in bed with him the next morning. Told her about him buying me breakfast, and us just becoming a couple after that. How it worked great as long as we didn't talk politics or history or about mom.

Sara wanted to talk more about that, how it didn't sound great at all. I didn't need her to tell me that. Mark and I had had problems since before we were even a couple, so what had happened yesterday had been a long time coming. At least I thought so.

So Sara told me how she worked as a dog-walker and about the crazy things she saw people do in the safety of their own homes. About Jake wanting to become a doctor but not daring to take the tests to enter because he felt he was cheating with his powers, so instead, he worked as a translator for a publishing company. Apparently, he was fluent in seven languages and was working on learning Japanese now.

Soon, I forgot everything that made me sad. I forgot about Connor, about mom, about magic and dreams and wendigos. My ghosts had gone silent, listening to us talk, and it was the sudden sadness of aunt Ellie that reminded me that we were drawing close to where mom grew up.

17

Just outside of Dartmouth, I pulled up the GPS on my phone and took on the job as a map-reader.

Loyde House lay another half-hour North-East of the city, which I hadn't expected.

"Is this a good idea?" I asked after we'd been on a dirt road for almost ten minutes. We had to go slow so as not to ruin Mrs. Hearth's little car.

"Why wouldn't it be?" Sara answered, squinting in hope of seeing something through the trees.

"How well do we really know these people? Maybe they're insane or something?"

"Don't think they're insane. For one, your mom always spoke highly of 'em, and for seconds, I don't think the province would let them continue taking in kids if they weren't doing a good job."

Just in case, I checked the reception on my phone, which was thankfully full. When I looked up again, the forest was opening up, and I couldn't help but stare.

A low stone fence ran to either side and around the farm. There was no gate, but an arch with some kind of family crest set in iron reached across the road. The road led to a parking lot shaded by tall oak trees, flower beds filled with the leftover from summer marked the perimeter. There was only one other car there, a minibus with the family crest painted on the side. Closest to the parking lot was a big, red barn, and behind that was a paddock where seven horses, one of them a foal, lifted their heads to look at us before returning to munching on the grass. Opposite the barn was another barn, this one with the double doors flung open so we could look into the interior, which looked mostly empty except for a few obstacles for the horses to jump. At the far end of these two, red buildings, lay a house. It looked Jacobean, if I was to guess at style, and was built with a pale stone. Smoke rose from one of the four thin chimneys jutting out from the roof. Just visible behind it, was a greenhouse. And there were actual hens walking around the space between the three buildings.

Sara parked and we stepped out of the car, and my ghosts flew out of the ceiling and stretching. I heard Eleanor complain that back in her day, carriages were much more comfortable, before the barking of a dog drowned her out. The twins ran toward the horses the moment they were out of the car, Magdalena following together with Elizabeth to make sure they didn't do anything stupid. What that might be, I didn't know. They were ghosts, after all.

I glanced at aunt Ellie, but she was again looking everywhere but at me. Her jaw was set and she was fiddling with her blond braid.

"Here goes," I murmured, and with Sara at one side and Eleanor and aunt Ellie at the other, I headed toward the house, trying to avoid the hens that had no intention of getting out of my way.

Something flickered past me and I stopped and turned. Two children were running along the stables, laughing. They didn't seem to notice us, and I saw they were dressed in modern winter clothes. Out of nowhere came a snowball and hit the boy in the lead in the head. He toppled over and fell into a snowdrift. The girl that had been chasing him was laughing, and an older boy came out of nowhere.

"What?" Sara asked, having stopped with me.

"Just memories," I said as I turned toward the house. T

he door opened and two men and a woman stepping out. They were well dressed and young, and walked straight past us, not seeing us at all, toward the parking spot, but I couldn't see any car waiting for them. When arriving, the woman turned to the two men and shook each their hands in turn.

"Congratulations. I think you will make wonderful fathers, and I'm so glad this worked out."

"We owe you everything," one of the men said.

"Don't say that," the woman said, patting his shoulder. "You're doing great things here."

Her words faded together with the memory, leaving a child dressed in summer-clothes chasing a cat across the parking lot.

Closing my eyes, I shook my head. "Many memories."

"Will you be ok?" Sara's hand on my shoulder was comforting and I leaned into it a little, drawing strength from her.

"Yeah, I think so."

Opening my eyes, I gave her a small smile and continued toward the house, making sure not to look at any of the many memories unfolding around me. At least it didn't seem to be any real ghosts here, which was good.

Before we were halfway across the open space, the front door opened and the barking dog flew out, not even touching the steps leading from the door and to the ground, heading toward us. It was shortly followed by a portly man clad in mostly greys but with a bright yellow and pink shawl tying a baby to his chest.

The hens jumped and sprang out of the way of the dog, wings spread and cackling like mad. Sara grabbed my shoulders, pulling at me, and the two ghosts flew forward as if to stop the dog.

"Boomer, sit!" the man roared and the dog flung its ass to the ground even before it stopped running, dust flew up behind it. When it stopped, it was still wagging its tail so much that it moved its behind back and forth across the ground.

Sara grinned and I giggled.

The man hurried forward, shooting the dog an exasperated look before reaching us and putting out his hand. "Elizabeth, so good to see you again. And who are you?" He'd turned toward Sara even before letting my hand go, and for a second, I thought of him as a tornado. The baby strapped to his chest was moving around, trying to take us both in with huge, brown eyes.

"Sara Hearth," Sara said, shaking the man's hand.

"Ah, a pleasure, a pleasure. I'm Micah Loyde, and this little guy is Tommy. Oh, and the fur-ball back there is Boomer. He loves humans, especially new ones, as we don't see too many of them up here. If he jumps, just turn your back on him and he'll stop. Welcome to our home."

After actually greeting Boomer, which was a wet experience as he really wanted to lick us all over, we went inside.

The house had that distinct musk of a home with a dog, mixed with the scent of babies; That milky smell that hung around them like a cloud. There was also a hint of both perfume and cologne, and wood smoke.

Micah led us into a den with well-used sofas and chairs and a chipped coffee table in-between. Logs crackled and burned in the fireplace. There were a few half-alive plants standing around, and pictures hung on the walls. A playpen made out of old, dark wood stood under one of the windows, and there was a dog-bed beside it.

From somewhere in the house, children's laughter sounded, but I was sure I was the only one hearing it.

"Make yourself comfortable and I'll get us that lunch, hmmm?" Micah said and was out the door before I had time to ask if he needed any help. Boomer followed his master with tail held high and a grin on his face.

"Is it ok to eat in the den?" I asked Sara, who was walking along the wall, looking at the pictures, not seeming to have heard. "What are you looking at?"

"These are all dated," she said, pointing at one of the pictures. "And named. I'm trying to find your mom."

"Oh," I said and glanced at aunt Ellie, that was still standing in the doorway. Her eyes were jumping around but stopped when they met mine. She drew a deep breath and stepped into the room. I wanted to reach out to her, comfort her, but something told me I wouldn't be welcome right now. She had her own grief to deal with. Instead, I stepped toward the wall.

The pictures all had the same setup. Micah and a dark-skinned man with straight black hair stood on the far side of a group of children of different ages and looks. It was clear that few or none were actually related, but they looked comfortable with each other. There seemed to be a picture taken every ten years or so, so most of the children appeared in two pictures.

The first picture I found with mom was of her as a teen. They were all outside and dressed for summer. Mom's hair reached past her breasts but had a sharp set of bangs almost hiding her eyes. She wore a yellow dress with a leather jacket over and had feather earrings in her ears and leather boots on her feet. Her grey eyes stared straight into the camera, her lips quirked in a half-smile I'd seen many times before when she was tricking Connor or me, or doing something she wasn't supposed to do, like sneaking me outside way after bedtime so we could drink hot chocolate together in the gazebo.

I was touching the picture before I realized what I was doing, and my fingers left a smear on the frame as I pulled them away.

I could see aunt Ellie's reflection in the glass. She was standing just behind me, eyes glued to mom's face.

"You found her?" Sara asked.

She'd taken a step back when I joined her at the pictures, giving me room to look for mom on my own. I wasn't sure if I appreciated it or not.

I cleared my throat before I answered. "Yeah. I think she might be fourteen or fifteen here."

I stepped to the side so Sara could see. Mom wasn't the only colored kid in the picture, but she was the only one with the look of the People, other than the other man. His eyes and hair hinted at the same roots as mom and myself, but his skin was more African.

"She looks healthy," Sara said.

I only nodded, moving to the next picture down the line. In this, she was four or five years old, and I soon found her in-between the others on the picture. This one was taken during the fall. Everyone were dressed in warm clothes with knitted hats and scarves. Mom and another kid a few years her senior were throwing leaves into the air and laughing while a girl looking to be close to adulthood was trying to calm them, but not able to stop smiling.

"They look really happy," I said before stepping back.

Aunt Ellie had pulled away. She stood by the windows, looking out at the grounds with her arms wrapped around herself. Eleanor was with her. The pregnant ghost had kept her distance until now, but she could clearly not let her friend suffer alone. Warmth filled my heart as I watched the two women embrace. At least someone could give aunt Ellie comfort when I couldn't.

Sara, sensing my emotional turmoil, reached out and squeezed my shoulder.

The clicking of claws on the stone floor announced Boomer's return seconds before the dog himself. He flew into the living room and almost bowled me over. Sara's hand on my shoulder the only thing keeping me up. Micah followed shortly after, a tray in his hands and Tommy wiggling in his harness to reach the clanking cups and plates on the tray.

I hurried forward and took the tray from the aging man before there could be an accident.

Panting, Micah thanked me and started untying the scarf holding Tommy in place as I put the tray on the table and set out teacups, bowls with sugar and milk and cream, small plates, a bigger plate with homemade scones with cream cheese and salmon, as well as a tea kettle.

"You were looking at the pictures?" Micah asked as he slumped into a sofa and put Tommy on the cushion beside him. The baby instantly tried to turn around, but Micah put a hand on his belly to keep him there. Boomer was standing with his head as far onto the sofa as he could get without jumping into it, licking the baby's fist.

"Yes," I said, sitting down, unsure if I should pour the tea or not. If there was one thing I'd learned from Mrs. Hearth when it came to tea, it was that they all had different times, and without knowing what kind of tea this was, I had no idea when to pour it to get the best taste.

As if reading my mind, Sara bent forward and drew in a sniff of the steam rising from the tea kettles snout. She nodded and leaned back on the sofa, looking toward the pictures again, giving me room to handle this the best way I could.

"Did you find your mother?" Micah asked, probably noticing my discomfort.

"Yes," I answered again, glancing at the pictures.

Micah followed my gaze and a wistful smile played over his lips. "Those were some good kids. I was sad to see them fall out of touch after moving out, but that's how it goes. People enter your life when you need them and leave when their job is done."

On the sofa, Tommy made a cooing noise and Micah bent over to talk to him. He seemed happy at the smile playing across the baby's face, probably thinking it was for him. I was the only one able to see Eleanor leaning over the sofa's back, her blond hair stopping just short of the baby's face. Tommy was staring right at her, and Eleanor was making silly faces. I hid a smile behind my hand.

Aunt Ellie was standing right behind her friend, smiling a little at the baby herself.

"Oh, how rude of me," Micah said, seeing my movement. "Just eat, and if you finish up, I have more."

Sara wasn't hard to ask and leaned forward, grabbing one of the scones and immediately biting into it. A groan of pleasure escaped her and I couldn't help roll my eyes.

"You made these?" she asked. Micah nodded, beaming with joy. "They're amazing."

For a time, the two of them talked about homemade foods,

17

Sara carefully touching upon the history of Loyde House every now and again. I listened, soaking up all the information I could.

Micah had inherited the farm after a car accident took his father and older brother, and his mother wasted away shortly after. He ran it normally for a while before meeting his husband, Eli. Together, they tried to adopt but weren't allowed. Instead, they became foster parents. Realizing that this was just what they wanted, they made Loyde House into what it was today. A kind of orphanage where there were always children ranging from newborns to eighteen-years-olds. To make sure the kids got the best childhood they could, they only allowed five or six children to live there at a time.

"We would love to save them all, of course, but then they might as well stay at one of the province-driven homes in the city. This way, we at least get to help some, which is better than nothing," Micah said before finishing off the last scone.

I breathed a sigh of relief that none of them had asked me to eat anything, even if Sara had glanced pointedly at my plate every now and again. Even if I was hungry, I couldn't bring myself to eat. Not now that I was here and so close to answers.

Aunt Ellie had moved to stand behind me. She was still hugging herself, but her sorrow was less now that she'd had time to get to grips with it. I couldn't remember her actually grieving mom after we came back from the Grey World, and this had to bring up memories and sorrows all of their own. Eleanor, on the other hand, had been talking for quite a while about how a lady should eat steadily to keep up her strength, and that I really needed to put on some weight if I ever wanted a man to take an interest in me. A man likes a woman with hips able to carry forth heirs, she said. I pretended I didn't hear her and finally turned the conversation to the reason we were here.

18

"So, Micah, we were actually wondering if you might know anything about mom's parents?"

Micah, currently holding Tommy on his lap and playing with his nose, looked up. "Oh, butternuts! I forgot to bring the file," he stood, lifting Tommy with him and holding him out to me. "Do you mind?"

"I... what?" Before I could think of a better response, he placed the baby in my lap, making sure to support his head with my knees.

"I'll be right back," and Micah was out the door. Boomer, who had lain down on his bed when it became apparent that neither of us would give him any attention, sprang to his feet and followed his master.

After a glance my way, aunt Ellie followed them.

Sara and I sat in silence and listened to the footsteps disappear deeper into the house. Eleanor fell to her knees in front of me and continued cooing to the baby, her eyes big and sad.

"Eleanor?" I said, making her look up at me with those eyes. "Would you mind going fetch the others? I want them close."

"Oh, ok."

"Thank you."

After a final coo at Tommy, she staggered her way back up on her feet, her belly almost hitting me in the face, if ghosts could interact with the living, and disappeared through the door after Micah.

"What was that 'bout?" Sara asked.

I shook my head, not sure how to explain it, not sure I even understood it. Sara seemed to understand anyway and leaned her shoulder against me as moral support. I pushed back.

Tommy started to whimper in my lap and panic coursed through me. Sara saw my hands flailing helplessly over the baby's face and reached forward, carefully lifting him off my lap, making sure to support the big head with her fingers. She sat the baby up in her own lap and started talking to it, making faces and weird noises. I leaned back on the sofa and couldn't help smiling.

"Can babies see ghosts?" I asked, watching Tommy grab at Sara's green hair.

Sara shook her hair toward the baby. "Dunno, but it wouldn't surprise me. Babies and animals see many things we don't."

I closed my eyes and allowed myself to relax for a second.

After a short time, Eleanor returned with the other ghosts. The twins spoke over each other about the horses and what they had seen around the farm. About the things growing in the greenhouse, and the hens. Magdalena was, as usual, somewhat more reserved, but when I asked her about what she'd seen, she blushed and told me about the foal that she liked. She'd always liked horses, she told me, which was why she befriended the stable boy back when she was alive. I couldn't help smile at her and want to hug her. Despite her somewhat rebellious nature after her brother was born, she seemed like such a sweet child.

Aunt Ellie arrived and gave a small coughing sound to warn us that Micah was on his way back, and the ghosts assembled themselves behind me, Eleanor making faces at Tommy while caressing her big belly.

"I am so sorry," Micah said as he entered the den, Boomer close at his heels. "I did find the file after we talked, then Tommy needed a change and I forgot about it and must have managed to put it away again before you arrived, but here it is."

He handed me a green plastic folder. On the front was a picture of a baby with honey skin and grey eyes, and a picture of a child, maybe five or six, with the same skin and eyes, then a teen, and finally a young adult. They were all of mom. Her name was written in marker just over the pictures.

"Are you really sure it's ok for me to read this?" I asked, suddenly unsure if I wanted to do it.

Micah shrugged. "Nancy is dead, and you're her daughter. I don't see why not. To be honest, it doesn't say much. It contains a copy of the letter that arrived with her, her birth certificate, and a few other papers that were mostly of interest to Eli and myself."

"There was a letter?"

He smiled faintly. "Yes, yes, but I don't know how much it will tell you."

I nodded and pulled out the papers within, my hands surprisingly steady despite the feelings moving inside me. Both Sara and the ghosts leaned closer. Even Tommy was captivated by the concentration suddenly filling the room.

The first paper was indeed a black and white copy of a letter. The writing was neat and small, and I guessed written by a woman.

To whoever will read this. This is my daughter. I cannot keep her and hope you, in your kindness and faith, will find her a good home.

She has gotten all her vaccinations and is healthy.
 Bless you

Another handwriting below said: *St. James United Church, Dartmouth, Halifax.*

I read the letter three times, making sure to hold it so the ghosts could read over my shoulder, before handing it to Sara.

At my movement, Micah hurried forward and picked up Tommy. I heard him ask if anyone wanted anything, and Sara asked for some water. With a nod, Micah was gone, and she turned to the letter.

I picked up the next piece of paper. It was a copy of mom's birth certificate. No mother or father was mentioned, and a post-it was stuck to it, saying that this was the certificate made after she arrived at the church, to make up for her not having one on arrival. The certificate was stapled together with another copy of a letter and a handwritten page. The letter was from the church if I was to guess from the signature of a Father Bradley on the bottom. It told of how they found the baby on the steps, lying in a basket and wrapped in blankets with the note stuck underneath to make sure it didn't blow away. Father Bradley believed the baby was a few days old, at least, and the doctor agreed. The handwritten page was just to say that the police investigation hadn't revealed anything. No one knew neither the mother or father of the child, so the province took her in.

I handed the certificate to Sara as I lifted the next paper, which was a copy of emails sent between Loyde House and Child Services in regards to taking in the baby, taking in mom. It seemed like Eli had read about mom in the papers and wanted to give her a home even before the investigation was over.

Seeing as the baby had clear First Nation blood, and Eli's own mother was a member of the Mi'kmaq tribe, they agreed without problem, and mom was sent to Loyde House just a week old.

I skimmed through the rest of the papers. They contained the newspaper articles from when she was discovered at the church, cut out and laminated so they wouldn't be destroyed, as well as her grades in school, yearly health updates, courses she'd taken. At the very bottom lay a few more drawings mom had made as she grew up as well as a few pictures. I flipped through them until I found one of my mom and aunt Ellie.

Behind me, the ghost made a choking sound. Pretending to stretch my neck, I shot a glance toward her. Aunt Ellie was turned away, hands in front of her face and shoulders shaking. Magdalena reached up and rested a hand on her elbow as I watched. Turning back to the picture, guilt filled my stomach at not being able to help. To have to keep them a secret.

In the picture, mom and aunt Ellie, looking to be in their late teens, were standing in front of a fountain, each with an ice cream in hand, grinning at the camera. They had one feather earing each, looking like they belonged to the same set, and they both had a blue leather bracelet around their wrists.

"That's your aunt, ain't it?" Sara asked, seeing me look between thin air and the picture. I nodded, not able to speak.

Micah returned and poured water with strawberries into two glasses. Tommy was in the playpen by the window, dozing, Boomer on the floor just beside him.

Clutching the picture, I looked at Micah. "Can I keep this?"

He reached out a hand and I handed it to him. He looked at it and smiled broadly.

"That was such a fun day, that one. And those two. They were thick as thieves, they were, practically joined at the hip. I was so happy when Nancy got together with that brother of Ellie's. That way, those two girls could be together forever." His voice grew thick and he cleared his throat, handing the picture back. "Yes, yes, you may."

I took the picture and clutched it to my chest for a moment. "Do you have anything else of mom's?"

Micah shook his head. "No, I'm sorry. She took everything with her when she moved in with your father."

"Oh."

Micah took a long sip of his water, brow furrowed. "You may want to visit that church, though. The one where she was left. I know she did a little digging both as a youth and before she had you. Most of our kids know who their parents are, even where they are, but Nancy never knew and was understandably curious. She visited that church many times, stopping by here on her way back or forth. Maybe they know something."

<h1 style="text-align:center">19</h1>

After drinking our water and using the bathroom, we said our goodbyes. Micah promised to tell me if he found anything of mom's hidden away somewhere. They had boxes of stuff from all their kids, after all, and mom may have left something behind that he didn't know about.

"Now what?" Sara asked as she slid into the passenger seat and shuddered. She'd just sat on Johana, who was yelling that she wanted to sit in front.

"If you don't mind, I really want to check out this church where mom was left?" I said after telling Johana to get into the back seat.

Sara only nodded, and I started the car. Micah was still standing in the middle of the yard, waving at us, with Boomer running around, chasing the hens. They sprang in every direction, and in-between all their golden brownness, a white bird took flight. I tried keeping my eye on it to see what kind it was, but it was soon too far away for me to see any details.

Giving one last wave, we left Loyde House behind.

I wasn't sure if I was happy or not with the visit. The picture I'd gotten was currently in the shadow-screen above my head, safe from crinkling in my pocket or getting damaged in my purse. Other than that and the name of the church, I didn't feel like I'd gotten much out of the visit. Still, it had been interesting seeing where mom grew up. I would have loved to see mom's room, but I didn't even bother asking as I guess they had to re-use the rooms for other kids as soon as the previous occupant moved out. It was clear Loyde House never stood still.

I could ask aunt Ellie, but not right now. There were so many emotions moving through her my own head felt like a rainstorm, every drop a new feeling hitting me in the face or burrowing through my skin.

Finally, I couldn't take it anymore.

Checking the rearview mirror to make sure we were out of sight from Loyde House, I pulled the car into a small pocket between the trees.

"What?" Sara asked, straightening in her seat as I unbuckled my belt.

"I need to talk to aunt Ellie," I said, aware of the sudden stillness from the ghosts. "Alone." I glared at the twins as they were about to climb through the roof.

"'bout what?" Sara asked. "And it's not like I can hear her side of the story anyways."

"I wasn't talking to you, but the others. I don't know, I just…" My words faltered as I met aunt Ellie's eyes. They were big and wet with unshed tears. "I just got to do this," I said and stepped out of the car, not even turning off the engine.

I'd barely taken three steps before aunt Ellie flew past me, pretending to jog but her feet barely touching the ground. She was so fast I had to run to keep up.

Soon, the trees swallowed the car, then the sound of the engine. Aunt Ellie tugged at the thread between us, wanting me to join her and at the same time wanting me to stay away, to be alone. She hadn't had any time for herself since she died, and now she finally did and she wasn't sure she wanted it.

"Hey," I panted, catching up when she finally stopped. "You ok?"

"Yeah, why wouldn't I be?" she answered, her back to me. Her hair was flowing around her head, a sure sign she was distressed.

"Because your best friend is dead and you haven't grieved her yet. You've had your hands full handling your grieving and selfish niece as well as a ga... a fright of ghosts that are both angry and happy at being back in the living world." I walked around her as I talked until I was finally looking her in the face. It was wet with tears that disappeared the moment they fell from her chin. "Because coming back here probably brought back a ton of memories that you would rather not have to deal with right now."

Her flickering eyes turned hard and she glared at me, her lips curling back from her teeth in a growl I could feel vibrating through my own chest. In the bush beside us, a bird squawked and took flight, almost hitting a tree on its escape from the sudden presence filling the woods.

"Don't," she said through clenched teeth, but her body was rocked by another sob and she curled into herself. "Please, don't."

"Aunt Ellie, I'm so sorry."

She screamed, the sound high pitched and sending a shock wave of sudden cold in every direction as she fell to her knees and buried her hands in her hair. I knelt in front of her, as close as I could get without actually falling through her.

"Now it's your turn. Now you grieve and I will watch over you."

She screamed again, her hands reaching for me but stopping

just short of my chest. I wrapped my hands around hers, careful to not quite touch her. I could feel the memory of her body heat touch my palms, and hoped that she could feel my heat as well. That she took comfort in it.

"As long as you need. I'll keep you safe."

Her hands flexed within mine and her breath hitched. Before I knew it, she was looking at me with big eyes. There was no sorrow there, only worry.

"You'll keep me safe," she said, words slow and heavy with thought. "You'll look over me."

"Yes. No wendigo will get you, even if I have to fight it myself."

Her faraway eyes snapped to mine, suddenly in the here and now. "But what about the others?"

"What?"

"The other ghosts, how will you keep them safe?"

I furrowed my brow, unsure where she was going. "I don't think the wendigo will know to look for them here."

"No, that's not it!" The world shimmered around her, the air suddenly hard to breathe, just like when I took control of the ghosts to banish Connor.

It felt like something hit me in the chest and I fell backward, landing on the sodden earth.

"Oh, no."

Aunt Ellie didn't say anything, but she was panting in fear, her hands now on the ground, fingers gripping the dirt like it was the only thing keeping her from floating away.

"The other ghosts," I said and she nodded.

Not caring about my wet ass, I crawled my way to my feet and started running back toward the car, aunt Ellie at my side.

"How didn't we think of that?" I asked between pants.

"How?"

"We didn't know," aunt Ellie answered, voice as steady as ever. "How could we know?"

"I should have known," I whispered as the car came into view.

It was still on, Sara sitting in the driver's seat. That was fine with me. I wasn't sure I could drive right now anyway.

Aunt Ellie shot forward, bundling up the youngest ghosts and almost pushing them into the car as I rounded the hood and threw open the door.

"We have to get back," I said before the door was even closed behind me. "We have to get back. Now."

"Why?" Sara asked, her phone still in her hands and open to a half typed text.

"Because of the ghosts, Sara! Because of all the ghosts I called out of hiding that are now wandering around, following me, ready for the slaughter when the wendigo wakes up again."

20

Sara was speeding down the dirt road, the small car jostling and bumping up and down at an alarming rate. In the back seat, the ghosts were talking over each other, my own fear and panic increased ten-folds by their own feelings. My head was chaos. My own feelings, theirs, the wendigo's hunger. Everything was jumping around just as bad as the car.

"Lizzie, talk to me," Sara said, forcing me to focus on her voice and the here and now. "What do you mean, there'll be a slaughter?"

"Ok, so until now it has hunted my fright of ghosts," I began, the ghosts in the back going silent to listen. "Because it could sense their collected energy or whatever from wherever it came from. But now, because I'm a necromancer or ghost-witch or whatever, I may have called more ghosts into the open. I don't understand it, but as Jake pointed out, I don't really know anything, but it seems the wendigo couldn't enter houses before, or it would have taken out all my ghosts." Sara was nodding. "And I guess it may not be strong enough for that yet, even if I don't understand the science of it. If it is a spirit, it should be able to walk through walls like my ghosts, right? So why didn't it? I mean –"

My hands were flying all over the place as I tried to describe my confusion at it all. Not seeming to care about the bumpy road, one of Sara's hands left the wheel and grabbed both of mine, forcing them to stand still.

"It isn't science, it's magic. It doesn't have to make sense," she said, her voice soft and calming. "But right now, we have more pressing matters, it seems. What's going on?"

I drew a deep breath and tightened my grip on her hand to keep from fidgeting. "The wendigo need to eat ghosts to get stronger. It probably can't enter houses yet. I don't think one ghost is enough to make it that strong, so my ghosts should be safe as long as they stay inside, but when I was fighting with Connor, I summoned more ghosts. I bound them to me, I can feel them, and they're out in the open, coming to me. If they stay in the open after dark, the wendigo can just hunt them down one at a time and get that much stronger that much faster."

"Yeah, that might be a problem," Sara muttered.

We turned off the dirt road and onto the small asphalt road leading toward the highway.

"I don't know how to fix this," I continued. "I don't know enough about this world, or this power, or anything," I glanced at the ghosts. "But this is my fault. It's my fault Sanderson died, and it's my fault those ghosts are out there, unprotected, and I have to fix it somehow, but I need help."

"What kind of help?" Sara asked.

I pulled my hands through my hair, wanting nothing more than to chew on my nails but trying not to. "I don't know. I don't really know anything about this world or my own powers. It's a lot to take in, you know?"

"I don't. I was born into this." Sara said, and I glared at her. "But I can guess. Even now, this whole shaman thing's pretty new to me as well." She chewed on her bottom lip for a few seconds. "From the top of my head, I think mom can help. Her crystals might be able to injure the wendigo."

"How? If it isn't even on our plane?" It could only touch and interact with ghosts, so wouldn't that go the other way as well?

"Magic," Sara said, waving her fingers at me. "Point is, she can help. She's dealt with things like this before."

"Really?"

"Not a wendigo, I think, but magic crises, which this is. She's one of the leaders of the coven, and that's what we do."

"One day, you need to sit me down and explain how the witching world works," I murmured, looking over my shoulder at the ghosts again. They were silent and scared, their fear running along the threads between us.

"But not right now," Sara said, speeding past another car. "Right now, we need to make a plan."

"How? I just told you I don't know enough about anything to make a plan!"

"You don't," Sara said with a grin. "But I do. Walk me through it again. Slowly this time."

I wanted to yell at her, to tell her that I'd already told her everything I knew, but before I could even open my mouth, aunt Ellie leaned past the seats and rested a hand just over my shoulder.

"Deep breaths," she said before drawing a breath through her nose. "And out." I did as she said, scowling all the while. "Now, from the top. She can help us."

"Lizzie?" Sara asked, glancing at me. I could just barely see her through aunt Ellie.

"Yes, sorry," I mumbled, drawing two more breaths before aunt Ellie leaned back, letting me look at the witch. "From the top?"

"From the top."

Sara and I talked and thought as she drove, my ghosts coming with suggestions or ideas every now and again but mostly staying silent. There was an argument between Elizabeth and Eleanor about us using witches to begin with. Elizabeth quoted the Bible but was soon shut down by all of us. Were any of the witches she'd met after coming out of the Grey World evil? She murmured something about Sara's powers but kept quiet after that. I wasn't sure what I would have done if she continued to argue. Leave her at the side of the road to walk home?

We were back within the hour, Sara driving like crazy, but I was restless and worried. What if we were too late? The sun would set soon and we needed to have all the ghosts tucked away safe by then. When darkness fell, the wendigo woke.

Finally, back at Mrs. Hearth's, Sara hardly had time to park the car before I was out of my seat and running toward the house.

I slammed through the front door, not bothering to take off my shoes, and ran into the kitchen.

Abigail was sitting at the table with a laptop open before her.

"Lizzie?" she asked, closing the computer. "What is it?"

"I need your help," I said, almost stumbling over my words in the hurry to say them. "We need to get all the ghosts to safety before the wendigo wakes up, and –"

"Slow down."

Behind me, Sara entered the kitchen. Putting her hands on my shoulders, she steered me into one of the chairs. "Breathe," she said. "And explain from the top."

I scowled but did as she asked, trying to stay calm as worry vibrated through me, but Sara had warned me that Abigail might dismiss me if I was too panicked.

"First of," Abigail said when I finished, not looking at us. "We don't know if the wendigo knows about them. If it doesn't, we don't need to stress this and can just let the ghosts come to us in their own time. Secondly, why is it your fault this Sanderson died? You couldn't know."

Something in her voice was different toward the end, but I couldn't put my finger on what, and right now I didn't care.

So I explained what I'd said to the ghosts earlier. How I should have helped them move on sooner, and if I'd done that, Sanderson would still be alive somewhere. "But I don't know how," I finished.

Sara finally sat in her own chair, having taken off my shoes and outer clothes and returned them to the hallway while I spoke. "Neither do we. Like I said in the car, maybe it's like in that show, *Ghost Whisperer*? They have unresolved issues with the living and you have to help 'em with that? But none of us knows. This is a whole new brand of magic."

I glanced at Eleanor and Magdalena. Elizabeth had probably gone off to find the twins. "If that's the case, we have a real problem. Some of them don't know anyone alive today except me."

I'd started picking on my nails, and Sara placed the saltshaker between my hands to give me something to fiddle with. She was pulling at her hair the way she did when she was thinking. Even Abigail seemed deep in thought, but the way she leaned away from me and kept glancing my way, made me think she wasn't thinking about the ghost problem.

Why were we just thinking? We had to act! But I was afraid I might ruin any chance the ghosts had of surviving if I opened my mouth, so I didn't say anything.

The heavy silence was broken as someone walked down the stairs, making the steps groan.

"I didn't tell you you could leave your room," Sara said as Jake entered the kitchen. "You're impossible."

She pushed out the chair on her other side with a foot and Jake sat.

"What's up?" he asked, his eyes jumping between us.

Without a word, Abigail stood and went to the fridge. Sara's smile died and she glanced at me. I sighed and told him what I was thinking.

When I was done, Abigail placed a plate with a sandwich in front of Jake. She wouldn't look at any one of us, which made me sad for some reason.

Jake ate his sandwich without a word, looking into nothingness much the same way he'd done while we were in the yard earlier. At least his eyes weren't running back and forth like he was reading. When he was done, he started tearing up what was left of his toast before he finally let the pieces go and looked up at all of us.

"First of all, we need to know if the wendigo knows," Abigail said. "I will not go out on some crazy ghost hunt if it isn't needed. Do you know what that would do to our reputation in this town?"

"And how do we do that?" Sara and aunt Ellie asked at the same time, Sara rolling her eyes.

"Lizzie has a connection to it, right? If we put her to sleep, she might read its mind?" Jake answered.

I shook my head. "If I nap, I dream of... other things, some in languages I don't even understand. The wendigo is active just before nightfall and during the night."

"Which is most of the day, now," Jake pointed out. "It will be dark soon. Having fed, it might not need as much sleep either."

"I can help," Sara said. "Like last night. If you wish to be inside its head, my powers might help."

"Yes, that might work. We need to know what it knows, and if it knows about the ghosts, we need to collect them somehow or protect them," Jake said, tapping one finger against the edge of his plate.

"How?" I asked.

"That I don't know. There are ways to bind a spirit. Maybe a protection circle?"

"So, what?" Abigail asked. "You want us to drive through town and throw up circles around all the ghosts out there? That's even worse than -"

"Or ask them to go inside, but yes," Jake said, interrupting her. "I'm surprised none has shown up yet, actually, one would think there would be a bunch of ghosts in these old houses."

I looked over at my own ghosts, who looked at each other, but this time Abigail answered before I had something to say. "That's because of Nancy. Mom said that after Nancy moved into the manor, she cleansed the area of excess energies and spirits." Her voice was hard, but I wasn't sure it was because Jake had interrupted her earlier, or from the topic at hand.

"What?" I spluttered. "Mom did that? How?"

Abigail shook her head. "We don't know. It usually happened at night, so mom thinks she did it in her sleep somehow. Which means you have that same power in you somewhere."

"But how do I tap into it? So far, I've only tapped into the ghost-witch or necromantic magic or whatever."

Abigail froze.

"Not true," Jake said, pointing at my chest. "You summoned your soul, as well. Maybe that's what we need to do." I raised my eyebrows at him and he shook his hand, as if pushing my question aside. "One thing at a time. Find out if the ghosts need protecting, and protecting them if need be, then see if we can't help you tap into your shaman powers."

"That sounds like a lot of work," I answered.

"And we don't have much time to do it," Sara added. "The sun'll be down soon."

21

No sooner than had we agreed on what to do next, Abigail stood and started finding dried herbs from the cupboards and boiling water. As she worked, she told me it would be Mrs. Hearth's sleeping tea, which we already knew from experience would work. Even for shamans.

As Abigail made the tea, Sara and Jake followed me upstairs, the ghosts like a silver river behind us. I was both surprised and not when Jake joined us in Sara's room, but he stopped at the edge of the bed as I sat on it.

"Is it ok if I join you?" he asked as Sara fell down beside me. "I will be looking into how to protect or help ghosts move on while you sleep, and Sara's magic could make it easier for me."

I shrugged and leaned against the wall. "Sure."

Jake smiled and sat at the edge of the bed, as if afraid to come closer.

Sara reached up and took my hand. "I told you we would figure it out, didn't I?"

"Yeah, you did."

"And this is a much better plan than what we thought of!"

I snorted. It was true.

"What was your original plan?" Jake asked, scooting a little farther onto the bed.

Sara grinned. "For Lizzie to use her necromancy powers to summon all the ghosts here in an instant."

"That's not all that bad," Jake said carefully.

"Yes, it is." I spat back, both offended and a little flattered. "I have no idea how it works. What if I summoned the wendigo as well? To a house full of ghosts? Or what if I did something worse? Like turn all the ghosts against the living? There's a reason you witches tell scary stories about necromancers, and I don't want to know why." I slumped against the wall. "Besides, did you see the look on Abigail's face when I mentioned necromancer magic just now? She's hardly looked at me since yesterday, and now I'm pretty sure she's afraid of me."

"Big whoop," Sara said, sitting up and bumping her shoulder against mine. "Mom's scared of everything she doesn't understand, so don't let her get to you. What she thinks doesn't matter."

I forced a smile to my face at her words, remembering saying the same to her time and again as we grew up. I hadn't known what mother and daughter were fighting about then, but I did now, and the words seemed to fit even better. Why should Sara give up her powers because some witch some time had let herself turn evil from the same powers? Using the same logic, why should I use my powers for evil just because other witches had done so before? I wasn't even a witch. Abigail should have given her daughter the benefit of the doubt, just like she should have given me the benefit of the doubt. She'd known both of us since birth, after all. She knew we weren't evil.

"There you go," Sara said, and I realized my face must have gone from sad to determined. "You're still you, and you're not evil."

I took her hand and leaned my head against her shoulder. On

her other side, Jake had scooted enough onto the bed to lean his back against the wall. He was holding Sara's other hand, and when she brought both her hands into her lap, our knuckles touched.

"Mom's afraid of the tree of us, and we've proven her time and again that we're not evil."

"We shouldn't have to prove it," I said.

"Amen," Jake continued, and I couldn't help my giggle.

He turned his head to grin at me, then leaned his head on Sara's other shoulder.

We sat like that until Abigail came in with a mug of steaming tea in one hand and a thick book pushed to her chest with the other. "Here," she said, handing me the cup. "Drink it up and go to sleep. I'll see if there isn't something I can do to help with the ghosts."

"Ok, thank you Abigail."

Without answering, not even looking at us, she turned and left the room.

Frowning, I drank the tea, still leaning one shoulder against Sara.

Before the mug was even empty, my whole body felt numb and I curled up on the bed. There was some fidgeting as the others found a comfortable position. Jake asked at one point if it was ok he lay like this or that, and I answered yes, too tired to think straight, and anyway, something about Jake was calming. Maybe it was him knowing so much and being so open about it. Maybe it was Sara's trust in him. I didn't know and I didn't care, but knowing that he knew what I was, was relaxing in a way I'd never managed with Mark.

In the end, Sara lay spooning me and we both rested our heads on Jake's legs. I'd gotten the lower legs, which were bony and hard, so I covered them up with a pillow and curled against myself. Sara lay on his thighs, her hand resting on my shoulder. As I slipped into sleep, I felt fingers move carefully through my hair, and another hand rested over Sara's hand on my shoulder.

Everything was dark, but as I tried to open my eyes, I felt something take shape around me. A body, too big and gangly to be my own. I tried twitching a finger but couldn't move. Fear rippled through me. What was going on? Why couldn't I move?

My body shivered and curled tighter, as if cold, and I felt sharp bones scrape against my fur. Fur.

Forcing myself to calm down, I let my senses work.

I was sleeping on hard stone. The smells slipping into my nose with every breath were stronger than I ever thought they could be. I smelled humans and animals. Sleeping and dead plants. Exhaust and garbage. There was blood, some hot and still running, some cold and spoiled. The sweet scent of death. And there was something else. A scent almost more like a sound in my mind than a scent. Like the twinkling of broken glass falling on stone. Or the sight of stars on the surface of the calm ocean.

Spirits.

Something recognized the smell, but it wasn't me. It was the same something that had moved the body earlier. The same something that grew hungry at the scent. The same thing with fur.

I recognized the mind now. Recognized the hunger.

I was in the wendigo's mind, but it was sleeping. When it was sleeping, I was still myself inside it, but I couldn't move its body, and for every moment I was here, I felt the hunger of it seep into my own mind and putting my own thoughts to sleep. Would I still be me when I returned to my body? Or was I really in my body right now, as I was in the wendigo? I had trouble thinking. I was so hungry. I...

Eyes stung with light of day, but it was faint. Moving about, body felt stronger.

Still hungry.

Needed more.

Still in dark of cave under den, nose rose and sniffed the air.

Was not far from spirit herd, but the smell of other spirits was stronger. Not weak as if they were inside a den. Something was different...

Sniffed again, then growled in contentment.

Different spirits. More than the herd. Many now, out in the open. Ready for hunting.

Crawled closer to opening with a growl. Sun was still out but would soon be down. Then it was time to hunt. Until then, sleep. Should not be awake at this time, but hunger was strong, and the smell made it more so.

So hungry.

Curled together, but could not close eyes. Was too excited about spirits. Could hunt and feed all night, and would be strong before sun rose again. A human body would be next, then meat and blood and...

I clawed my way out of the dream. It was like moving through syrup, but I could feel sleep slipping away and I was grateful. We didn't have much time. Especially not if I'd been inside the wendigo for as long as it had felt.

"Hey, Lizzie?"

Sara. My muddled mind gripped onto her voice and I used that awareness to pull myself closer to the surface.

With heavy eyelids, I managed to blink. The room was bright with the orange light of the setting sun.

"No," I whispered, the shock of it making the last of sleep burn away. "No, no, no."

I sat up, feeling hands slip from my hair. It looked like I'd been sleeping with my head in Sara's lap. Jake was nowhere to be seen.

"How long until sundown?" I asked.

"Just over an hour," Sara answered

"Fuck," I mumbled and pushed out of bed. "We have to go. It knows. It could smell the other ghosts, and it knew. It knew that they would be enough. After tonight, if we don't do anything, it'll be strong enough to possess someone." Jake, Abigail and Mrs. Hearth stood in the door, probably having heard me wake. They looked grim. "Please tell me you've found a way to protect ghosts?"

Abigail gripped the box she was holding tighter as she answered. "There are some, but we will need you to help us find them." I noticed Jake and Mrs. Hearth were both wearing backpacks.

"Ok, then," I said. "We don't have long. It was really close to us, so we should head toward the closest ghost and work our way outward from there. Maybe we'll make it."

The others only nodded. We were all on our way down the stairs when Abigail turned to me. "Do you know where the ghosts are?"

The others stopped and turned to look at me as well.

"Close," I said, touching the cold spot at my sternum. "I can feel them and know in what direction they are, so I should be able to lead us to them."

Abigail set her jaw and turned, heading down the stairs. Her mother, daughter and Jake following close behind. I was a little slower. My own ghosts circling me.

"It will be too slow," aunt Ellie said. "You should split up."

"We can't. Only I can see you, remember? The others might walk right past ghosts without knowing it."

"Can we not help?" Jonathan said.

"Yeah," Johana said, nodding vigorously. "We could go out and find the ghosts. Try to talk them into a house or something. If they do not want to, you send someone our way to put protection around them."

We were at the bottom of the stairs and I turned, looking up at the ghosts gathered there. "No. The wendigo knows your scents. It doesn't mind what ghosts it eats, and I won't risk more of you."

"That's not your choice to make," aunt Ellie said. "If we want to, we can help. Let us."

"I can't... what if the wendigo finds you and eats you?"

"We know it's out there now. We know we are in danger. We can go two and two if that helps."

I looked at Magdalena, hugged against Elizabeth.

"Lizzie, you coming?" Sara called from the door.

"Yeah, just a sec," I answered.

"We don't have time!"

A frustrated growl escaped my throat, a lot like the one the wendigo had let loose, and I closed my eyes. "I don't want to put you in danger."

"You are not. It's our choice," aunt Ellie said, and I could feel her hands on my shoulders. "Let us help."

"Lizzie!" Sara again.

"Fine!" I exclaimed, unsure who I was actually answering. Stepping out from under aunt Ellie's hands, I moved backward toward the door, locking my eyes with hers.

"We'll go toward town," she said hurriedly, as if afraid I'd change my mind. "There are many ghosts there we can talk to, and many places to hide."

"Fine. You go two and two. Check in with me every time you find a ghost, ok? If it doesn't want to or can't listen to you, tell us where it is and I'll send someone. Just... be really careful, ok?"

"We will."

"And if either of you doesn't want to do this, stay here. Your partner will stay with you. Maybe some ghosts will show up and need explaining, ok?"

"Ok."

"Just... be careful."

"You too."

Sara helped me into my coat and was pulling me out the door even as I tried stepping into my shoes. I glanced back. My ghosts were standing at the bottom of the stairs, backs straight and chins held high. Even little Magdalena looked fierce, despite holding hands with Elizabeth. And then, just before the door closed, they seemed to disappear. As I crawled into the front of the car, I couldn't help but wonder if I'd ever see them all again.

22

As we drove, I told the others what my own ghosts were up to. Abigail argued that they would be in danger, that I was selfish to let them go, and I argued that I'd argued that same point, but it got me nowhere. When she didn't get anywhere with that argument, she changed gear.

"But what if the ghosts there don't listen to them? Or can not listen to them? What if your necromancy command is too strong?" This last she said with a sneer.

I turned, trying to catch her eye, but she was glaring out the front window, avoiding looking at me. "Then they'll tell me and we'll turn around. For now, this has a much better chance of working."

"How do you know? You don't know anything."

We argued on, a feeling of heavy dread and sorrow forming in my stomach as we did. Why couldn't she look at me? Why was she fighting me on everything I said and did? Where was the warm woman I grew up with?

In the middle of Sara trying to calm the both of us, I gasped. A man was standing in the middle of the road, our mirror just missing him as we zoomed past. He didn't seem to care, but he turned with us as we passed, always looking at me. A thread in my chest turned back to stay with him.

"Stop!"

Jake hit the brakes as he swung to the side.

Before the car was even still, I was out the door and jogging toward the ghost. He'd turned and walked after as we passed him, and the wonder I saw in his eyes turned to anger.

"What the fuck's going on?" he growled. Knitting his hands, he walked faster. "What the hell do you think you're doing?"

I stopped. "Sorry?"

"Dragging me out here like this! I don't listen to your kind. Never have, never will." He was in my face now, spit flying at me and leaving chill trails through my head. He looked me straight in the eye. "A half breed too. As if that makes it any better."

"Ok," I took a step back so I didn't have to lean away from him but could look straight at him. I was the tallest of us, and when he realized, he hunched his shoulders, as if ready to hit me. "You won't hurt me even if you try to hit me. You're a ghost." He snarled. "And I'm here to tell you you're in danger." He spat again. "There's a wendigo. At dark, it'll come outside and try to eat all the ghosts it can find. When it's sated, it will be strong enough to possess a human, and then it will hunt for meat."

"That's not my problem," the man said and spat yet again. I made a face. He was super gross. "Wendi-whatevers are your shit, right? You people probably summoned it and so it's your fucking problem."

I closed my eyes for a moment and drew a deep breath. "I don't really care what you think, but the wendigo will hunt you down and kill you."

"Can't kill me. I'm already dead."

It was getting harder and harder to stay calm. I did not have time to argue with this guy. "It will absorb your energy and there'll be nothing of you left. I've seen it happen before. It's really painful. So get into a house or I will have to go to extreme measures."

He crossed his arms and looked me up and down. "Like what?"

Without taking my eyes off him, I yelled for the witches. As soon as they reached me, I pointed out where the ghost stood. While he was yelling at me, Mrs. Hearth moved around him, making a perfect circle of salt. The moment her mother closed the circle, Abigail hurriedly put out four stones, one at each point of the compass.

"What the fuck are you doin'?" the ghost asked as the two women finished and headed back to the car. "Hey, I'm talking to you!"

He moved to follow, but the moment he tried stepping over the salt, it was as if he hit an invisible wall. Seeing this, I breathed a sigh of relief and turned, jogging toward the car. The ghost was yelling for me to come back, but I didn't bother turning and closed the door on his slurs.

"What was that?" I asked, looking at the two witches in the back seat.

"Salt works as protection," Mrs. Hearth started.

"And staurolite should hide him from the wendigo," Abigail finished, keeping her gaze fixed out the window. "I charged them as much as I could. It's the best we can do on such short notice."

"Won't it all be disturbed by the next car coming by?"

"No. The salt is sealed with magic, and the stones are sealed to it again. They will stay until we come to remove it again," Mrs. Hearth answered.

"Thank you," I said, leaning back in the seat. "Next one is that way."

"So who was it?" Sara asked, leaning her chin on the shoulder of my seat. "The ghost, I mean."

"Didn't know him," I answered.

"Why did you get so angry?" I turned my head to look at her, and she shrugged. "Grams told me."

I rolled my eyes and turned forward again. "He was an open racist."

A tense quiet filled the car. It held until we were well out of the inhabited areas and heading into the forest, when Jake's phone buzzed. It lay in the middle console; it's light flashing twice before going dark again. He didn't even look at it, but it reminded me that I had turned the sound off on my phone at breakfast and not looked at it since. Sure, I'd seen the heap of lost calls and messages when I looked at the map to get us to Loyde House, but been too busy even to consider checking them out. Now, though, I had no excuse.

I had over twenty missed calls, most from Connor, one from Erik, my boss, and four from Mark. There were seven unheard voicemails; six from Connor's number, and one from Mark's number.

My stomach knotted and I followed the instructions on the message with Mark's number on it. As I waited for the automatic female voice to finish her greeting, I started chewing on my thumbnail, not caring if I ruined what polish was left.

"*So I guess you've turned off your phone,*" Mark's voice said. "*I'm not sure if it is to avoid me or what, but I'm guessing it means you need time, and I'm going to give it to you. I know I said yesterday I wouldn't be here when you were ready, but that's a lie. I won't leave you while you're going through something. I might not know exactly what it is, but I want to help."* He took a heavy breath. *"If this isn't something that's been a long time coming, if this is just you grieving, it's not enough. A momentary feeling is not enough to end us. I hope you'll call me back when you hear this. We'll figure this out. I love you. Bye."*

I lowered my phone and stared at the shining screen for a moment, feeling angry and relieved all at once, before one of the threads in my chest twitched from in front to beside me, grabbing my attention.

"Wait, there's one here! Stop."

Jake pulled over and I jumped out of the car. Sara was just behind me with a backpack over one shoulder, and we headed into the gloomy pine forest.

"Connor?" she asked, staying close to me and lifting her black coat to keep it from tangling in the fallen branches and underbrush.

"No. Mark."

"The boyfriend that wasn't the best friend?"

"Yeah."

"What did he want?"

"One sec."

In-between the trees I saw movement, and a young girl stepped into our line of sight. She wore a summer dress, was barefoot, and had a flower crown on her head that made her look like a fairy.

"Hello?" She said in a light voice, stepping even closer. "Can you see me?"

"Yeah, hi," I said, crouching to be closer to her eye level. "Who are you?"

"I'm Malia," she said, not able to say the R in her name. "Why can you see me?"

"Hi, Maria. I'm Lizzie. I honestly don't know why I can see you, but I can, and I'm going to ask you something, ok?" She nodded. "Do you know anywhere you can hide when the sun goes down? There's something bad back in town and I think it might hurt you if it got the chance."

"Why?"

"Because it eats gh... girls like you."

Her eyes grew wide before she looked over her shoulder again and smiled. I swear I could hear singing, but her voice drowned it out. "That's ok. As long as I stay in the folest, they'll plotect me."

"Who?"

"The women in the tlees. They came a few nights ago and found me. They ale leally nice, even if many of them ale going to sleep and not waking up again until summel. The othels say that is nolmal and they'll all be asleep soon."

"Ok?"

The little girl shrugged. I guessed she was seven years old, and I wondered for a moment how she died, looking the way she did. "Even when I had to walk, they followed me."

"Had to walk?"

She nodded quickly. "Yes. Out of nowhere I had to stalt walking but now I don't. You know why?"

"That's my fault," I said, looking away, shame coloring my cheeks. "I made a mistake and called you to me, but now that I've found you, or you've found me, I don't think that should be a problem anymore."

"You sule? I don't have to walk anymole?"

"No, I don't think so. Just let me try something."

She nodded.

I closed my eyes. Concentrating, I felt for that cold spot

within me. I could feel all the different threads connected to me, most of them leading back to town, a few into the forest around me, and one pointing straight at Maria. That thread was drawn tighter than the others and felt almost hot when I found it. I pictured it snapping, but nothing happened. Then I pictured myself cutting it with a scissor. That felt more right and the cord thrummed but didn't break.

At that moment, the owl flexed its claws. They were wrapped around that cold spot, as if holding it in place, and I got an idea.

Instead of trying to break the cord myself, I pictured my owl doing it. It was clear in my mind as it bent down and snapped its beak around the warm thread. The moment it clicked shut, the thread broke and disappeared into nothing.

Maria giggled as if I'd tickled her, and I opened my eyes.

"How do you feel?" I asked.

"Ok. It felt funny, but not anymole."

I smiled. "I think that should do it. You should probably go back to your friends now and hide for the night, ok? And maybe try to find a hiding place for when the winter comes and all the women are asleep, ok?"

"Will you come back?"

The question caught me by surprise and I opened and closed my mouth a couple of times before I was able to answer. "Yes, I will try. If not, I live back toward town, in one of the old Victorians, you know them?"

She shook her head, looking sad for a moment before she smiled again. "But I can find you anyway. I can feel you." She touched her chest at that.

I couldn't do anything but nod and stand. "I have to go. Say hi to your friends for me."

"They alleady know," she said with childish certainty before she turned and skipped into the forest. Again, I was sure I could hear singing, and I thought I saw something move in there, welcoming Maria.

"Is it gone?" Sara asked, making me jump. I'd forgotten she was there.

"Yes," I said, turning to her.

"What did you mean by friends?"

As we made our way back to the car, I told her about Maria and the friends she'd talked about. When I mentioned the singing, Sara started pulling at her hair. I wanted to ask what she was thinking, but we were at the car and I let it go as we both crawled in.

"How did it go?" Jake asked as he pulled out of the spot where he stood and turned to follow my pointed finger.

"As well as it could, I think," I answered. "It was a little girl, but I was able to – "

My words were cut off as I screamed, making Jake yell out as he swerved to avoid what he couldn't see.

"Don't do that!" I continued, swatting at Johana, who was standing in the middle of the dashboard, her face centimeters from mine.

Her eyes were huge anfd her grin wild. "I did not know I could," she said.

"Who don't do what?" Jake asked, face pale and eyes flying across the road to see what I'd screamed at.

"It's Johana," I said. "One of my ghosts. She's standing in the middle of the dashboard. Sorry I scared you. What?"

"Talking to me now?" Johana asked.

"One would think, you being from an era where kids were supposed to respect their elders, that you would respect me," I mumbled. "Yes, I'm talking to you."

"Jonathan sent me," she said, as if not hearing my mumble even if I knew she could. Her grin told me so. Blasted nine-year-old. Always so cocky. "We have found a group of ghosts now, and the others have as well, but they cannot do anything but walk."

"Why?"

"They do not know. Earlier today they felt a stab inside their mind, then it was like something took over." She looked away. "It was the same we felt when you took us over in the street. You did not let them go as you did us."

I stared at her for a moment before I started nodding. "So all I need to do is let them go, right? Then they can do what they want?" Johana nodded. "Ok, thank you! Go back and tell the ghosts that as soon as they feel they can, they should hide."

"Why?"

"I'm going to release them."

Johana nodded again before she blinked and was gone in a wisp of almost white mist.

"What was that 'bout?" Sara asked, and I told them. "Do you even know how to release them without seeing them?" she asked when I was done.

"I let Maria go. It was different than letting my fright go, but I did it, and I should be able to do it even if I can't see them."

After a short conference, Jake swung us off the road and onto a dark forest road. There were few houses out here, and few people that could see whatever might happen. As we drove, we passed another of my summoned ghosts, but I didn't tell the others. If I was able to release all of them, it would be free soon enough.

The car parked and off, I let the witches lead me into the woods.

The sun was still up, throwing fiery light everywhere it could reach, but the forest was dark. There was a hint of the fire to the shadows surrounding us, but despite the only trees with cover left were pine trees, the gloom was absolute. Like we'd stepped from one world into another.

"Explain this again?" I said as they found a suitable spot. I didn't see how it was different than the other places we'd walked past, but the witches all agreed, so I wasn't going to argue.

"We'll use our gifts to empower yours. That way, you should be able to feel every spirit you control and it should be easier for you to focus on letting 'em go," Sara explained as Mrs. Hearth found a stick and started drawing things in the clean dirt, going clockwise. Meanwhile, Abigail was putting stones at each point of the compass, just outside her mother's circle.

"Ok," I mumbled, feeling the tremble in my voice more than hearing it.

We stood there, Jake, Sara and I, and looked on as the two women prepared. When there was but a little opening in the circle, they waved us forward without a word. Jake gave my shoulder a reassuring squeeze before he turned and kissed Sara. I was already in the circle by the time she joined me.

We sat down as we'd been told, facing each other, Sara holding my hands. The two witches closed the circles. First the inner, then the outer.

I hadn't expected to feel anything. Magic circles and the like were just fairytales, after all. What I'd seen back with the ghost was nothing more than that, a fairytale affected by another fairytale. But when the first circle closed, I felt something. It was like a trickle of water against my skin, and I swear I could smell Mrs. Hearth's herbs. Then Abigail closed the stone circle and I felt something crash over me, more like a wave than a trickle this time, and it felt like I was vibrating.

Sara blinked and her eyes went from blue to yellow. I could almost see her power flicker around us. A golden mist that spread until it hit against the shimmering walls of the inner circle. Sara herself was flickering. Her hands in mine grew younger and then snapped back to themselves. Her hair did the same, jumping from her short, green pixie cut to the long, black she used to have, then the long blond she had before she started dying it.

A smoky scent snuck its way into my nose and I turned to look outside the circle. Mrs. Hearth had lit a bundle of herbs and was moving with the clock around the circle. She was flickering as well. Her yellow eyes were locked on me, but I saw how her face changed around them. It grew younger and prettier, and her broken nose straightened. I saw the ghost of her wedding band on her finger, then the ghost of tears on her face and heard the memory of the screams she let loose as she birthed her two daughters. Then came the pain when her oldest disappeared.

Sara tightened her grip on my hands and I turned back. She cocked her head, asking if I was ok without words, and I nodded that I was, even if that was a lie. There were so many ghosts in this forest. Memories of young people laughing and partying. A baby crying. And there were the ghosts of every living person here. The memory of the person they used to be, their strongest emotions and the most important moments of their lives. It was hard to focus with it all.

Then I felt a tug at my sternum. One of the ghost pulling, screaming, dying.

I was out of time.

23

Closing my eyes, I took a deep breath and focused on the spot at my sternum. That point where all the threads connected to me . They were real, and there were real people at the end. People that were in danger because of me. People I had to save.

But there were so many distractions down here.

Even with my eyes closed, I could feel the shifts of the living people around me. Seeing the ghosts of who they once were and who they hoped to be. Seeing the ghosts of those most important memories that made them the people they were today. And there were the ghosts of the forest around me. The memories of teens in love sneaking away from their parents. Of families hiking. Further back were the memories of the men that built the road. Or men cutting some of the trees for one reason or another. And then there were women. Young girls, really, sneaking into the woods with their newborn bastards and leaving their babies in the forest. I could hear the children scream and scream until they froze to death, left behind by their mothers, nameless and forgotten.

I couldn't think down here.

The owl moved in my chest, and without a word, I knew it could help me. I let it, and it felt like I fell out of my own body. Like I fell upwards.

Wind tore at my hair and I opened my eyes. The sun blinded me and I turned my whole body away, looking at the dark horizon to the east. The wind wasn't pulling at my hair but at feathers. White owl feathers covered my whole body, and I knew I was up in the sky in the shape of my owl. I was hovering, wings spread, on a warm breeze. The light of the sun was too bright for my eyes, but as long as I had it at my back, I was ok. The feeling of this body was both familiar and unfamiliar. Like I'd been this owl before but had forgotten. Tentatively, I flapped my wings and knew instantly how to move my feathers to stay in one spot.

Below me, blowing like streamers in the wind, were a multitude of threads, glimmering like moonlight on the dark, still ocean. Most of them were tied around my claws, but six of the threads was connected to my chest, and they were much wider and stronger in color than the others, and braided into those threads were other ribbons of a light grey, like fog, and bright yellow. The yellow was the color of a witch's magic. The grey I'd never seen before, and I hadn't time to wonder about it even if I wanted to. The sun was setting behind me, the world growing steadily darker. The wendigo had already taken out one ghost, probably one wandering too close to its hiding place, and it would be a massacre if I couldn't somehow release the other ghosts before the sun was down.

The threads were spread in every direction but most led back toward town.

I moved my feathers and flapped my wings until I was even higher. The wind was cold and hard against my body. I squinted my big eyes and looked toward town. I could see it now, behind a carpet of green. To my left was the ocean, crashing against the shore with sounds my owl ears could pick up but my human ones had no chance at noticing.

Focus!

Being in this body was so familiar, so freeing, it would be easy to lose myself to it. To just give up on all the responsibilities of my human life and go hunting for tonight's meal. There was much prey in this forest. I could live comfortably. No more hurt. No more heartache.

Heartache.

I shook my head, which made me tip over for a moment before I righted myself and focused on the threads. Mrs. Hearth had said that magic wasn't good or evil; the user decided how to wield it. But I was new to this. Strong emotions triggered my powers, and in that moment, when I saw Connor and pushed him away, I wanted to hurt him. So my magic reached out the only way it knew how.

But that didn't help me figure out how to release all those hundred ghosts I'd tied to me. How had I even done that? With rage and hurt and even a little hate. That was the feelings that controlled me when I saw Connor and his new family. And sorrow. I'd already been broken by mom's death, and he broke me yet again. So I needed the opposite of those feelings to set all the ghosts free.

I needed hope and love and forgiveness.

Forgiveness. Connor's face flashed before my rounded animal eyes, but no. I couldn't forgive Connor. Not for what he'd done.

His face was replaced by that of Cornelia. His baby daughter. My baby sister. Resentment coiled in my stomach, and I realized what it was. I was angry at the baby for taking my father away from me. That he got a new chance with her, and that she would get the man I'd grown up with for herself. That he left me for her.

But that wasn't true.

He'd left because mom got sick, and he didn't take me with him for whatever reason. I was sure he had an excuse, but Cornelia wasn't in the picture then. Her parents didn't even know each other. So I couldn't continue being angry at the baby. Honestly, a small part of me wanted to get to know her.

The coil of resentment tried to bury its fangs in my flesh, tried to hold on.

I flapped my wings and looked closer at the wound it left, seeping with pus.

Catherina, the woman who had born my father his second daughter. The woman that resembled my mother in so many ways. I resented her for keeping Connor away. Maybe, if he hadn't met her, he'd have come back. When he left, he said he needed time to think, then he met her and chose to stay with her. If he didn't meet her... But no, Connor would just have found another woman instead of Catherina. Another excuse.

The coil turned to a snake in my mind, and it hissed, throwing all its might against my thoughts.

Connor had said she knew about mom and me, that she knew the man she was with were married and had a grown daughter somewhere in the same country. What kind of woman did that to another? To a daughter?

The snake hissed, coiling around the light that was my forgiveness.

But my anger wasn't with Catherina. She'd fallen in love, if the pictures on their Facebook pages could be any proof. One couldn't help who one fell for, and I didn't know what Connor had told her about his marriage, about his family. Maybe he hadn't told her before she was already pregnant and she couldn't get away. Maybe he'd lied when he said she knew about us. Catherina wasn't to blame in this. Had never been.

The snake tried to smother the light, but it burned ever brighter, seeping out between the coils.

One couldn't help who one fell in love with, but one could help what happened when one fell out of love. Mark had never been to blame for all of this. Even if he had somehow made me stay in Toronto when Dr. Altman called, the curse would have caught up with me. But I'd hurried to leave, not only out of love for my mother but for a need to get away. My love for Mark had long since rotted away, leaving nothing but friendliness. That first night he was in Sky Harbour, our last night as a couple, was the best sex we'd had in months. I'd poured all my fear and anxiety into it, burned all that energy, and it had been great, but that spark that once burned between us was long gone. He still loved me, but I didn't love him and I resented him for it. I blamed him, but it wasn't his fault. I was to blame. So I would forgive him.

The snake hissed in pain as the light burned its belly.

In my chest, my broken heart started to mend. Just a single stitch, but it was enough for me to really notice the damage.

Mark hadn't done this. My heartache went much deeper than that. It was mom.

My owl form screeched against the evening wind, the sound swallowed and hidden in the darkening sky. It was the sound of an animal in pain. An animal thinking it was dying.

Mom had died. How could she leave me like this? After everything? She'd given her life for me, but it would have been better if she didn't. I would remember her loss, but she wouldn't have known I'd died.

But she'd done the one thing she knew how to do. She had a

moment of clarity, released for a moment from the clutches of her own personal curse, and she made a choice. She saved me. The least I could do was forgive her.

So I did.

The snake burned away to ash. Ash that seemed to fall from my white owl body to be swept away by the wind.

Mom's face flickered before my eyes, and I heard her laughter, and her voice singing my lullaby, and smelled her perfume of lavender and paint, and felt her fingers carefully comb through my hair.

Mrs. Hearth's face followed. Sara, and Abigail, and Emma, and the other people that had helped raise me. I remembered the friends I'd grown up with and loved, the people that had always had my back, and the light in my chest grew until it filled all of me, and I knew, instinctually, that this was my own power. Not the powers that had made me control all the spirits for who knew how big a radius, but my own power. The power belonging to the owl. In the same way, I knew what to do next.

With another screech, this one of a hunter taking down its prey, I flew straight up in the air. The sun kissed my feathers and made the threads catch fire as they streamed behind me. As the momentum faltered, I tipped backward and threw out my wings, taking a backflip and leveling out at the last possible moment. The threads loomed before me like a wall of moonlight before I flew through them. They clung to me like spider silk.

With a push, I threw the light of my power out before me. It slipped from my skin and feathers like a scythe. I closed my eyes and sent out one simple command.

I release you.

The threads snapped like they'd been cut with scissors and floated toward the ground. Long before they reached the treetops, they crumbled into dust and were blown away by the wind. As if they'd never existed. The six threads leading to my own ghosts were still there, as clear and strong as they had been before I released the others.

Now, still gliding on a current, I looked at them. Two of them, connected to the twins, were in the direction of my house. Two others were close together, moving closer to the twins. Those were Eleanor and Elizabeth. But the threads leading to Magdalena and aunt Ellie were apart, as if they'd walked their separate ways, and they weren't drawing closer to home at all. They were still in town.

Worry gnawing in my stomach, I started circling down toward the forest. I could feel my body down there, calling. Despite my wish to fly off to hunt for tonight's dinner, I still had work to do as a human. Soon, I was just over the trees, and with knowledge I didn't know I had, I made my way between the sharp autumn branches and into the golden glow of Sara's power.

I looked down at myself, seeing my pale face and my hands clenched in hers, then I blinked my eyes, and for a moment, I was in both bodies. The owl hovering above me, and the human sitting on the cold ground looking at Sara. She was still flickering. Then I was back inside myself. Looking up, I saw the owl was gone.

Before me, Sara cocked her head in question, and I nodded. Letting my hands go, she closed her eyes. The aura of gold pulled into her. When she opened her eyes again, they were her normal blue.

Outside the circle, the other witches must have seen, for as soon as Sara opened her eyes, Mrs. Hearth started putting out her incense, and Abigail moved counter-clockwise, picking up the stones she'd dropped. The moment she lifted the first stone, it felt like a veil was lifted from my body and the living shapes stopped flickering. I could still hear the babies crying as they died, but when Mrs. Hearth pointed her stick at the point where she'd started to make her circle and then followed in her daughter's footsteps, the cries faded as well. My body felt lighter, my bones as hollow as the owls, and a headache was building behind my eyes.

The forest was dark now, the only light that of the flashlight on Jake's phone, and even that seemed too much for my aching eyes. Like I'd taken the owl's eyes with me.

"How'd it go?" Sara asked and helped me to my feet.

A small smile trembled over my lips. "I did it."

For a moment, everyone stood frozen, then Sara gave a small yelp of joy and threw her arms around me.

"That doesn't mean the danger is over," Jake said when Sara calmed down enough to stop jumping around with me. She turned his way, arms still around my neck, and stuck her tongue out at him. He and I shared a smile at her childishness, but his died within seconds. "The wendigo could still come after your ghosts, or there might be others still wandering the streets. We have no idea how strong it is. We need to find a way to banish it back behind the Veil."

I was about to ask what the Veil was, but Mrs. Hearth talked over me. "Lizzie needs to rest. She is exhausted."

I didn't bother to ask how she knew.

Abigail spoke up next; "We should head back anyway. The house is warded, so I can do more to protect the ghosts there."

"Thank you," I managed and she gave a small nod.

I couldn't be sure in the dark, but it felt like she wasn't looking at me at all. She hadn't looked at me since she learned what I was.

Sadness moved in beside the worry, but I was too tired. Leaning on Sara, I let her help me toward the car. Jake lifted my other arm and lay it over his shoulders. I almost didn't have to walk at all, the way the two of them were supporting me.

As we made our way through the dark forest, I kept checking on the threads still connected to me. Eleanor and Elizabeth were close to home if I was to guess based on the proximity between them and the twins, but aunt Ellie and Magdalena were still separated in town. What were they doing?

Reaching the car, Jake let me go and hurried ahead to open the passenger door for me. Sara helped me in, and I slumped into the seat. The cold of the night had started to fill my hollow bones, and I turned on the seat warmer the moment Jake started the car.

Without another word, we left the woods and turned onto the road leading back to town and home.

25

I was exhausted, so I tried sleeping a little on the way back, but sleep was slow in coming. At least to me. I knew the owl was sleeping inside me, but I didn't know how I knew or what it meant. This was all too new, and there was no one close that knew enough to help me. If my search for my grandparents didn't pan out... What should I do? Should I go to an indigenous reservation and ask after their shaman? What if they turned me away? What about my other powers? Would they know how to help me control what Jake called necromancy, or would the shamans do like the witches had done in the past, and kill me just because I had that power? I didn't know, and I was too tired to think about it.

My eyes were closed, and my forehead rested against the cold window. I could feel myself slipping away, slipping through darkness, and...

... opened my eyes to the dim light of an alley that smelled of seawater and beer.

I tried looking around but couldn't even move my eyes. Or, I could move, I was moving, but not of my own will.

My body was small, that of a child, and I was crying. Blond hair fell into my eyes when I stumbled on stockinged feet, but I managed to stay up.

There, I could hide there.

Panting, I hurried behind the steel stairs and crept as far into the shadows as I could. The asphalt was wet and cold and hard against my naked knees and hands as I crawled my way inside, but it was distant. I could feel it, but it could not feel me.

"Magdalena!" The realization that I was inside her mind almost jarred me awake, but at my voice, she froze, and I managed to cling on.

"Miss Lizzie?" she whispered.

I tried to answer, but it seemed I'd lost my ability to talk to her. I could feel the fear coursing through her, and I almost woke up. I could feel her hands trembling in the puddle they rested in and her lower lip vibrating as she fought not to sob. I was afraid she didn't know I was there, but she continued speaking as if she could still feel me.

"It is here, Miss Lizzie. The wendoggo. I saw it and I ran, but I think it followed me. Help. Please, help…

I cursed as I woke in the car. My own fear at her words must have woken me, like a nightmare.

Sara was touching my shoulder. "What is it?"

"We have to go to town," I said, turning toward Jake.

"What? Why?" he answered, not taking his eyes off the road. We weren't far from home, I noticed.

"Turn around! Magdalena's in danger!" Mrs. Hearth said something in the backseat that sounded like a cry of alarm, but other than that, no one reacted. "Magdalena has lost aunt Ellie somehow, and she said she saw the wendigo. It's in town, and she thinks it's following her. We have to go back."

"How do you know?" Jake asked.

"I just do!"

When he didn't turn immediately, I lunged for the wheel.

Sara sprang forward and grabbed my wrists. I was still weak and tired from the ritual in the woods, and she was so much stronger than me right now that I didn't even try to fight her.

"Please," I whimpered, hearing Magdalena's voice through my own.

Jake glanced at me before he made a U-turn. The car behind us honked angrily but Jake didn't pay it any mind and sped down the road.

"Thank you," I whispered, not hearing Magdalena anymore, but I could still feel her so I knew she was ok.

"I was going to turn," Jake said in a calm voice that reminded me of the one adults used on panicked children. "I just didn't want to do it in the middle of traffic."

I only nodded and fell back in my seat. Sara let my wrists go but was still leaning between the seats, as if ready to grab me should I try to attack her boyfriend again.

"Where is she?" she asked now, trying to smooth things over.

"At the marina," I said, closing my eyes and trying to remember what I'd seen in the dream. An alley. She'd hidden underneath a set of metal stairs. That could be anywhere, but as I'd entered her mind, she'd glanced over her shoulder and I'd seen the docks, the glinting ocean black beyond them. "There weren't any big boats there, but a few motorboats, so I'm guessing the north side of the marina, where you can rent spots, you know?"

"I don't," Jake said. "But you'll lead me. Don't worry. We'll get there in time."

I hoped so.

My eyes still closed, I tried to reach Magdalena, but I couldn't do it. I could feel her fear, remembered the feeling of the wet asphalt under her feet and knees and hands, but I couldn't enter her mind again. I was too afraid to fall asleep, so I was stuck in my own body. Cursing under my breath in frustration, I opened my eyes and stared out the window.

We were on the road going through another part of the forest that surrounded Sky Harbour. This one was younger and less dense, and soon we would enter another residential area with more modern houses than our own, and we wouldn't be far from town after that. Maybe we could actually make –

I screamed as pain roared through my head. Crumbling into myself, I gripped my skull with both hands, feeling the nails dig into my skin, but that pain was nothing compared to the one that was flaring through my head, my throat, my chest.

Inside me, the owl awakened and started moving restlessly. Outside, I could just barely hear the others in the car yell for me to tell them what was going on. Most of all, I heard the rushing of my own blood in my ears, and aunt Ellie's roar of anger and fear as she was doing something.

My own scream died, but I was still clutching my head.

"Lizzie! Answer me!"

Sara. She was touching me, sitting almost on top of me. Opening my tear-filled eyes, I saw she somehow had made her way between my legs. She was sitting on the floor under the dashboard, gripping my face in her hands. Her eyes were flickering gold, but not in the way of her using magic, more like she was fighting to keep it back.

"There you are," she said when I met her eyes, forcing a smile to her lips. "What's going on, can you tell me?"

"Aunt Ellie," I managed before clearing my throat and trying again. "It had her for a moment. I could feel it pushing its claws into her throat, shoulder and head. Could feel it feeding on her."

Sara glanced at someone behind me, but I didn't dare look away from her face, afraid the pain I was still feeling would overwhelm me again.

"You said 'had'?" she asked when turning back to me.

I nodded. "It isn't feeding on her now. She's still alive, so she must have gotten away from it."

Sara nodded and used her thumbs to caress my cheek. "We're almost there. Jake's driving like cray-cray." I could feel it. The speed we were going at, the way we turned corners, the yells and honks from outside trying to slow us down. "We'll be there any moment. What do you want us to do?"

"I don't know. I can feel them, can go to them. I need to help them, Sara. I can't let it happen again."

"Shhh, I know. We know. We'll help you, ok? Somehow, we'll help you and your ghosts."

Jake's hand came out of nowhere and supported Sara's head. "Hold on," I heard him say, and Sara braced against my legs and the seat.

The brakes screamed and the car slid forward. When it stopped, it was so sudden it felt like my organs would fly out my mouth. By the time I'd swallowed them back down, Sara had unbuckled my belt and someone had opened my door. Mrs. Hearth reached in and helped me out, Sara following close behind.

If I'd been tired before, my body felt like it was in a coma now. The pain in my chest was growing stronger, and the tugging at the threads between me, aunt Ellie, and Magdalena were so distracting I kept forgetting how to move my own body.

We were at the edge of the marina, as close as we could get

with a car. I took a stumbling step forward and almost face-planted on the gravel. Mrs. Hearth was still holding my arm, holding me up. I could feel her magic wash over me. She was trying to keep me calm but even that wasn't enough to keep me focused on my own body.

"Here," Jake said, kneeling before me, offering me his back. I slumped onto him without a word and clung on as he stood. "Where to?" I pointed and he took off at a jog.

If this had been the weekend, the marina would be full of people enjoying the view before it was too cold to walk along the ocean, but it was a weekday, so we were as good as alone. Good thing, for I wasn't sure what people would think if they saw us.

A young man carrying a limp, young woman on his back, closely followed by another young woman with green hair and a knee-length black coat. Walking somewhat slower but still keeping up, Abigail dressed as a modern-day forty-year-old but carrying a carved wooden box, and her mother in a long, purple dress and a bright red jacket. There was still a leaf in her white hair from our trip into the forest.

The thought of us made me chuckle weakly, but no-one noticed.

The docs were dark, the bulbs of the streetlamps smashed, glass littering the ground. The only light came from lamps higher up on land and a few lights down by the boats. Every now and again, glass crunched under our boots.

We reached the area where I thought Magdalena would be, and I asked Jake to slow down as I gripped her thread with my mind and tried to follow it.

"There," I said, urgency in my voice.

The opening to the alley was almost hidden by shadows.

The alley was made up of the space between two historical wood buildings. One of them was a small office of some kind but was locked and abandoned for the night. The other was a bar, not open on weekdays.

Just inside the alley, the aura of darkness and hunger hit me and I groaned, my vision going blurry for a moment before I saw movement ahead.

"Miss Lizzie!" Magdalena's voice was thin and scared.

I squirmed until Jake let me go and I stumbled off his back. I'd barely taken a couple of steps forward when someone came hurtling, back first, out of the darkness.

Aunt Ellie flew right at, then through, me. I shuddered as I felt the wetness of her last breaths in my own lungs, then heard Sara gasp as aunt Ellie passed through her as well.

Fumbling in my pocket, I drew out my phone and turned on the flashlight. The sounds of rustling fabric behind me told me at least one of the others was doing the same, but I didn't need more light to see.

The alley was a dead-end, opening into a small courtyard in-between ancient wooden houses and one brick wall at the back, blocking off whatever exit once upon a time was there. The steel steps Magdalena had hidden under led up to a door in the brick wall. The asphalt was cracked and littered with puddles of who-knew-what and broken bottles. It stank from the dumpster standing behind the house-turned-bar.

In the middle of it all, seeming too big for this closed-off space, stood the wendigo. It was just as I remembered it from my vision of Sanderson's death, but somehow it seemed even bigger now. Hunched over, moving on all fours as it was, it was still taller than me. The bristling fur on its back and legs was wet and slimy, sticking to the black skin underneath. Its animal-skull head was at the same height as my chest, but it was turned away from me.

It was stalking toward the stairs, where I could see the white of Magdalena's nightgown. She was huddled up against the brick wall and her face shone with tears in the weak light from our phones.

"Are they safe?" Sara asked from behind me, and I shook my head, unable to answer.

At her voice, the wendigo stopped and turned. The claws on its fingers scraped against the asphalt, the sound making my teeth ache. It didn't have eyes, but I was sure it was staring right at me. It cocked its head and took a step toward me. Somehow, recognition moved over its faceless skull. Cocking its head back the other way, it let out a hissing growl, a mix between canine and feline.

"What was that?" Jake whispered.

No one answered. No one could.

The wendigo drew ever closer.

I wasn't sure what I was doing. I needed to keep it away from Magdalena and aunt Ellie. Where was she anyway? Why hadn't she come back after being flung away?

"Magdalena?" I said, my voice making the creature freeze just two steps from me. I didn't look away from it, keeping its eyes locked with mine. Maybe, just maybe, it didn't understand what I was saying and I could get the ghosts out of here. Right now, it shouldn't be a danger to the living.

"Yes?" Her answer was low and shaking, and the wendigo made to turn away.

I tightened my grip on the phone, which was shining it right in the face, and the movement stopped it.

"Do you know how the twins move about?"

"They walk?"

"They can move by willing it as well. Johana showed up in

the car earlier. Do you think you can do that? Do you think you can try and will yourself back to the house?"

"But what about Miss Ellie?"

"I'll take care of her."

"Are you sure?"

"Do you trust me?"

"Yes."

"Then try."

The wendigo had taken another step forward, and this time I took a step back. This close, I could taste the rotten meat on its breath and feel the hunger gnawing at my own stomach.

"What's going on?" Sara hissed in my ear, and it took all my concentration not to scream and look away from the creature. I'd forgotten she was there.

"I'm trying to get Magdalena to leave. Aunt Ellie is behind me somewhere. You think your mom could trap the wendigo the way she did the ghost?" I answered through clenched teeth.

Sara had taken a step back with me, the hand that wasn't holding her phone pulling Jake with her. Without answering, she disappeared from my sight, but I didn't dare look away from the creature.

I was sure the wendigo was glancing after her, wondering what was going on, as it steadily came closer. My legs weren't as long as its were, so it came a little closer with each step.

"Magdalena?" I asked. "Talk to me."

She sniffed before answering. "I cannot do this, Miss Lizzie! I do not know how."

I was just at the edge of the alley now. I could feel aunt Ellie close by, and the fact that she wasn't moving around, wasn't talking, wasn't fighting, scared me. My head, shoulder and chest still hurt, and so I could guess that she was hurting as well. When I spoke next, my voice was colored with that pain and worry, sounding harsh and angry. "Magdalena Elizabeth Key, I need you to concentrate and *get back to the manor now!*"

The feelings pushed from me and along the thread binding me and the young ghost together. Too late, I realized what those feelings would do. That I'd given a command. But before I could speak, Magdalena was gone. I felt her thread shift and she was together with the others.

The wendigo stiffened, as if noticing the disappearance of its nightly snack, and roared.

Dizziness assaulted me, and the sound of the roar fueled my headache. Legs wobbling, I took hurried backwards.

The wendigo reared up on its hind legs, and as I hurried away, it slammed back down.

"If you have any way to trap it, do it now!" I yelled.

Hands grabbed me around the waist and swung me away. One crystal flew by on either side of me. The wendigo, still hissing, swung at them but missed.

The crystals hit the ground at the same time and stopped right where they hit, not bouncing or rolling as stones normally would, and started to glow. The wendigo roared again and threw itself forward, but it hit against an invisible wall.

My legs gave way and I would have fallen to the ground if Jake hadn't kept me up.

"By all the chroniclers of the world," he whispered. "I can see it."

The wendigo was pacing in its small cage, just barely touching the invisible walls with one claw as it moved around and around.

"I think we all can," Abigail answered, her voice toneless. "Why can we see it?"

"It's feeding on the magic in the stones," I answered, pushing away from Jake and looking around.

"How do you know?"

"I can feel it getting less and less hungry."

"What?!"

"Abigail," Mrs. Hearth said in a hard and low voice. "Not now."

"But she is bound to it! Like she summoned it! How can..."

I tuned her out as I hurried out of the darkness and closer to the water's edge. I heard steps following but didn't care who it was. Crouching on the edge of the dock, I stared into the water.

Aunt Ellie lay just under the surface, as if she didn't remember how to float. Her eyes were closed and her mouth open. She couldn't drown, not again, but something was wrong, I just didn't know what.

I stretched toward the water, thinking to draw her out of it, but she was too far away. Trembling now, I crawled out on the support beam cutting between the different slots. Both the boats that used to stand here were up for the winter, leaving them open. When closer to the water, I reached down again.

The water was cold and burned my skin, but I didn't pull back as I reached in up to my elbow. As my fingers sank into aunt Ellie's arm, she opened her eyes and looked right at me. That was when I realized what was wrong.

I could see the bottom through her eyes, the broken bike half-hidden in the sand and seaweed and the car tires, and I could see my fingers inside her arm. Not only that, but she seemed greyer, somehow. I'd thought it was just the water, but I could clearly see a difference between my hand inside and outside of her. The understanding of why this was happening came to me slowly, like it wasn't my own thought, but sent through the thread between us.

Aunt Ellie was dying.

"What're you doing?" It was Sara. She had crawled out on the beam after me, making it wobble under my feet and almost tipping me into the icy water if not for her hands on my shoulder. "We have to go."

Her voice was vibrating with fear, but I couldn't look at her. Couldn't look away from the woman in the water. Aunt Ellie looked so pale, so weak.

"Can you move?" I asked. She shook her head in answer, her blond hair floating and hiding her face for a few seconds. "Can you wish your way back to the manor? Like the twins and Magdalena?" She closed her eyes but didn't move, like she didn't have the energy even to shake her head. "I don't know what to do. I can't leave you here. Aunt Ellie? Please?" She looked at me with eyes the same blue-green as Connor and myself.

"Lizzie." Sara again.

Without waiting for an answer, she reached out and grabbed my elbow, pulling my lower arm and hand from the water. My skin was as pale as hers, not my normally warm color, and my nails were blue and purple. She wrapped my hand in hers and blew on it, the heat burning more than the cold but I didn't flinch, didn't even look away from the ghost in the water.

Couldn't. If we left now, the wendigo would get her.

Inside my chest, I felt three of the threads shift. They were at the same point where Magdalena had been just seconds, minutes, hours, before. It felt like forever I'd been sitting here, watching my aunt die.

The threads shifted again and I heard a splash just behind me. The sound was so unexpected that I turned, seeing the three youngest ghosts standing in water to their waists. Magdalena had her arms wrapped around Johana's hips and was almost completely submerged. When she saw aunt Ellie, however, she let Johana go with a little cry and sprang to her, straight through me and the beam.

"What happened?" Jonathan asked. "Little Elizabeth came back, crying and screaming for help, saying that the wendigo had killed Miss Ellie."

I shook my head. "Not yet, but I think she's..." I couldn't bring myself to say she was dying, but the boy seemed to know it anyway.

With a tight jaw, he nodded once and moved through the beam and Sara, who closed her eyes hard and continued breathing on my hand. I couldn't quite feel it anymore.

The twins took one of aunt Ellie's hands each and closed their eyes while Magdalena cradled the older woman's head in her lap, sitting cross-legged on an invisible surface. The three young ghosts shimmered the way Johana had done in the car, then aunt Ellie did as well and they were all gone. Their threads were together with the others, and I breathed a sigh of relief, sagging on the beam and almost toppling into the water.

One of Sara's hands flew out and grabbed my neck. Not hard, but enough to make me remember where I was and find my center again.

"What happened?" she asked.

"They're back home. I hope at your place, but I can't tell from here."

"Ok, good. Then we can go as well. Come on; I'll crawl up first, then you follow. You can tell us what happened in the car, where we can heat you up."

"I –"

"Lizzie, I know things are rough right now, that a lot's going on and you're tired, but we can't stay here." She glanced over her shoulder with those words, and I saw that the three others were standing there. They all stood with their backs to us, but Abigail kept glancing at us over her shoulder. "The wendigo's almost free, and we can't be here then. It's too strong."

"We can't just leave it."

"We don't have a choice. We don't know how to fight it."

I wanted to argue. Wanted to tell her that it might be strong enough to possess people now, that leaving it in the middle of town would give it ample choice. But I also knew we couldn't fight it. Until just now, I was the only one able to see it. For all I knew, it was still more spirit than not and only other spirits could fight it. We could just hope it was stuck in the cage until dawn came and it didn't have time to do any harm.

"Ok," I finally breathed, and Sara slumped in relief.

Carefully, she crawled up the beam and her mother helped her onto the dock, turning away from me and whispering. I moved to follow, but my hand was like a big chunk of ice, hardly usable, and I almost slipped off the beam three times before I was at the dock. Sara and Jake were there; both faces grim and angry as they helped me to my feet. Mrs. Hearth and Abigail were a few boat-slots away, mother with a firm grip on her daughter's arm, her face as angry as I'd ever seen it.

As if feeling my eyes on her, the old woman looked my way and her face softened. She said something to Abigail, not as angry this time if I was to judge, but her daughter only pulled her arm out of her mother's grip and stalked toward the car. My stomach coiled at the turned back and the slumped form of Mrs. Hearth.

Without a word, Jake swung me into his arms and Sara placed my frozen hand against his chest inside his jacket. At the touch, he squealed like a mouse, then glowered at his girlfriend but he didn't ask me to move it, and the heat of him slipped through my cold skin, seeming to banish some of the pain. I rested my head against his shoulder and let him carry me to the car.

Just once did I glance back, and I saw the glow of the crystals in the dark of the alley, but not the wendigo. I could feel it looking at me, though, the hunger like a cloud around the alley opening, but it was still trapped.

Abigail was already sitting in the driver's seat in the car. Mrs. Hearth sat behind her daughter, and Jake carefully lowered me into the back seat. Mrs. Hearth took my head and laid it in her lap, stroking my hair. Sara climbed in after me and put my feet across her thighs. Jake took the passenger seat, and without a word, Abigail started the car and drove away.

I must have fallen asleep as we drove, for I woke in the familiar turns just below the hill leading up to our houses. I didn't remember dreaming anything, just the feeling of being in a dark wood, but no fear or scary things.

Mrs. Hearth was still stroking my hair. Sara's hands rested on my lower stomach, still cradling my right hand in both of hers, warming it. The water in my sleeve had spread to the fabric at my stomach and I now had a big, wet, cold spot there as well. Thankfully, that coldness had stayed on my skin and not slipped into my muscle and bone and blood, to spread through my body. My chest was still warm, where the owl was once again sleeping. The cold spot that connected me to my ghosts didn't seem quite as cold anymore, but more like a stone or necklace that has lain in a chest for some time before being used. Not quite cold, but chill none the less.

In the front, someone cursed and Abigail said in a low voice: "Is she awake?"

"Yes," Mrs. Hearth answered. I'd known her my whole life, and she's used that same polite but clipped tone with me when I'd done something she strongly disagreed with. The thought of Abigail being in trouble with her mother almost made me giggle, but it wasn't really funny. Just my tired brain. I honestly felt a little drunk.

"Well, you can tell her that her father's here."

Those words banished the giggle deep into my stomach, where it was pulled apart by a sudden burst of dread. Why was Connor here? Was he going to argue about the house now? I didn't have the energy for him, or anything else, right now. I needed to find aunt Ellie and see if she was ok. I needed to figure out if I could save her somehow. Then I could sleep, and after that, I might find it in me to deal with Connor and his stupid ego.

Mrs. Hearth must have noticed my change in emotions, for she stopped stroking my hair and turned my face toward her with both hands, stroking my cheeks. "Do not worry, dear. I'll have a talk with him and you do whatever you need to do, ok?"

I nodded.

Abigail turned us into the driveway and stopped the car. Doors opened and people crawled out. Sara helped me up and out, and when I turned to look for Connor, I saw Mrs. Hearth already marching across the road to our house where he'd parked.

Not meeting his eyes, I turned away.

28

Abigail marched to the house and up the steps, unlocked the door and disappeared through it without looking back, hugging her box to her chest.

Sara kept an arm around me, hand at my hip to keep me beside her, and moved us steadily toward the door, Jake on my other side, as Connor started talking to Mrs. Hearth. It was a struggle to not glance over my shoulder as we moved. I was curious if Connor would try pushing past Mrs. Hearth. He'd always respected her, but never as an equal.

We were at the top of the stairs when he called my name. When I stopped but didn't turn, I heard him talk in a low, angry voice to Mrs. Hearth, and I took the opportunity to slip into the house.

"I'll find one of grams' teas for you," Sara said, almost handing me over to Jake before she disappeared into the kitchen, boots still on.

Abigail was nowhere in sight, but I heard her moving around upstairs. For a moment, I stood listening to her footsteps before something moving along the threads between me and my ghosts made me move deeper into the house. Jake followed close behind, his arms out, as if afraid I would fall and ready to catch me. I was tired, but my whole body had reached a stage of numb where I didn't feel pain or tiredness. Not unless I let myself, and right now, I didn't.

"Aunt Ellie?" I asked as I entered the sunroom before stopping in the door.

Aunt Ellie lay on the divan by the biggest window. I could see the dark green fabric through her skin and bathing suit, making it look like she was actually underwater. The fact that her hair floated around her head didn't help the impression.

The other ghosts were around her. Eleanor was sitting in a rocking chair beside the sofa, Magdalena in her lap, rocking steadily back and forth. The older woman was humming in a low tone as Magdalena clung to her chest and sobbed. The twins were on the floor, still holding aunt Ellie's hands in their own, and their big sister Elizabeth had wrapped her arms around them, trying to give comfort. They knew, as surely as I, what was happening. Or they feared it as much as I did.

At my voice, aunt Ellie opened her eyes, and the others turned to look at me. Aunt Ellie smiled at me.

It felt like I was floating, just another ghost, as I walked through the room and fell to the floor at her side.

She lifted the hand Jonathan had been holding and rested it against my cheek. Normally, I could feel the memory of her touch, but it wasn't there anymore. There was so little of her left. I tried touching her hand, but my own slipped right through it and landed on my cheek.

"What can I do for you?" I asked.

Her voice was far away, as if she was deep underwater, which was only fitting. "Nothing," she answered. "There is nothing to be done."

"But what's happening?"

She rested her hand on her chest. It was shaking, as if holding it up to my face had been too much of a strain. "I think I might be dying."

"Please, no. I need you, I..."

Her eyes turned hard. "You don't. You are a strong woman in your own right, and you don't need any of us."

"But I don't know what's going on."

"Neither do we, but remember what you promised? You promised to let us move on. You have to do that for me now."

"No."

"Yes. If you don't, the wendigo will come here and it'll get me. It'll kill me as it killed Sanderson. Is that what you want?" I shook my head. "Oh, Lizzie. I know your heart is already broken, and I am breaking it even more, but this has to be done. We can't stay here forever, and you know that."

"But you might get stronger. You might be better tomorrow, and then we can fight the wendigo for real and send you on properly."

"We both know that's not going to happen," aunt Ellie said, a small smile on her lips.

I was crying, the tears burning in my cracked cheeks. Abigail was rushing around upstairs. Sara appeared by my side and slipped a warm mug of herbal tea into my hands. It burned my frozen skin. The ghosts were standing in a semi-circle around aunt Ellie and me. In the hall, Mrs. Hearth was talking loud and angrily as the door slammed shut and Connor called for me again.

Aunt Ellie closed her eyes and sighed as only a younger sister could. "That boy always had the worst timing."

Connor marched into the sunroom, his shiny black shoes clicking against the wooden floors. Mrs. Hearth was just behind him, saying something about him having no right to barge in this way. The land might be his, but the house was hers.

He stopped in the door, looking at Jake, Sara and me sitting on the floor. The rocking chair was still moving weakly after Eleanor and Magdalena sitting in it. His eyes flew around the room before landing on me again.

I turned away from him and back to his sister, my aunt. She needed me now.

"Sara, I need you," I said, setting the mug on the floor between us.

"'course," she answered, taking my hand before it reached my lap. "What'll you do?"

"Elizabeth, look at me when I'm talking to you," Connor said, making all the other Elizabeth's in the room turn but me.

"Mrs. Hearth, can you please get him out? I really don't have time for him right now."

"Yes, dear."

"No. No ''yes, dear'', here. I'm here to talk to my daughter, who is treating me with less respect than I ever raised her to do." I heard him take a step into the room. "Now, listen to me. You've been nothing but rude toward me since you called and I..."

His voice trailed off as I turned to look at him. I wasn't angry or anything like that, but I was tired and focused and knew what I needed to do. Maybe it wasn't the right way to make someone move on, but I didn't know anything else. I could feel my necromancy powers roiling off me in cold waves now, matching the cold spot on my stomach and the hand still resting in my lap. Somehow, Connor was sensing it as well, or maybe he saw something new in my eyes. I don't know, and I don't care.

"I don't have time for you right now."

My voice was as steady as it had ever been, but there was an echo there. An echo coming from the Grey World where I'd been held when I died. Where this power came from. I could almost see the grey mist creep along the floor.

Connor stood frozen, and when he didn't say anything else, I turned back to aunt Ellie. She was lying still, but she'd grown even weaker. She was more an outline than an actual person now, but her eyes were clear and they were looking at me with a mix of pride and fear.

"What are you going to do?" she asked, her voice vibrating along the thread still keeping her alive, or whatever she currently was.

"I'm going to command you to move on."

Her eyes grew wide before they narrowed and she smiled. "I always liked a challenge."

I couldn't help but smile back before I turned to Sara. "I need your luck now."

She nodded and took a deep breath. As she let it out, her eyes turned to gold.

Jake reached over and took the cup from between us and drew away, and I turned back to aunt Ellie.

"If this doesn't work..." I began, but she shook her head.

"No time for that, Lizzie. I don't have the time, and neither have you. We both know that."

I nodded and closed my eyes. Fixing her face, her voice, and the feel of her in my mind. Then I filled in the room around those things with what I needed her to do. Finally, I opened my eyes and looked straight at her. The cold of my necromantic powers was running wild, reaching into the room like vines after sunlight, but I gripped it and turned it to aunt Ellie.

The misty grey power curled through me then around the

thread leading to aunt Ellie. When it reached her, it curled around her as well.

"Elizabeth Josephine Key, Ellie among friends and family," behind me, I heard Connor gasp and take another step forward. "Aunt Ellie. I command you to move on. I command your spirit to travel to its next natural destination, whatever it might be."

Aunt Ellie closed her eyes and a grimace of pain sprang across her face before it relaxed. The mist had her tight in its grip, and then she was gone. Just... gone.

My hand fell out of Sara's and I felt her stop her magic. My own magic was reaching around the room, but I pulled it close and wrapped it around me like a blanket. Didn't want to let it touch my other ghosts. For all I knew, I'd just killed aunt Ellie. But no, I couldn't think that way. I'd done what we both knew had to be done. I'd find another way to help the others, one that was more secure and proven, but for now, I'd done my best.

I drew a shuddering breath and let Sara help me into the rocking chair where I curled up. Jake returned with the tea and I hugged it to my chest, breathing in the steam and warming myself as best I could.

Just as I was about to close my eyes to rest, Connor said: "Ok, someone tell me what is going on here, right now, or I call the police."

Mrs. Hearth sighed, but before anyone had a chance to answer, the door slammed open and Abigail screamed from the hallway.

The scream was cut short as something thudded against the wall, followed by the heavy sound of wood against wood and the clattering of stones.

Sara shot to her feet and was moving toward the hallway, Mrs. Hearth close behind. Jake was on his feet as well but didn't follow the women. Instead, he was heading toward the stairs. That left only Connor and me in the sunroom. He'd turned at the noise, but now he was turning back to me, his face pale and angry.

"Elizabeth," he began.

"Not now," I managed and pushed to my feet. My legs were wobbly under my weight and my hands hurt.

"Yes, now. I have a right to –"

He was cut off by my scream.

The chronicler had just reached the foot of the stairs when something big and dark came flying from the hallway. It hit Jake in the side and pinned him against the wall, its claws digging into the paneling and pressing so hard he grimaced.

The wendigo growl-hissed in his face, putting its skull up against his forehead. After barely a heartbeat, it roared in irritation and flung its victim to the stairs. Jake hit hard but was able to catch himself. Feet scrambling, he crawled up the stairs as fast as he could. The wendigo turned toward the sunroom.

For a moment, we locked gazes and it was like we knew each other. Then it looked at the ghosts standing around me, and lastly, it looked at Connor. It crouched, moving its haunches like a cat ready to spring at its prey.

"No!"

I reacted on instinct, and the grey glow I'd wrapped so tightly around myself flew out and tied itself to the threads connected to me. I saw the mist reach for the windows, reach for all the ghosts I'd bound to me once before. Before the word was even out of my mouth, the owl was awake in my chest. The light I'd felt earlier was there, and with it, I was able to pull the mist back around myself. It unwrapped from the threads, but my wish had still thrummed through them. I could feel the fear in my ghosts, but also the resolution.

The wendigo jumped.

We surged forward.

My ghosts, of their own free will, slammed into the wendigo, grabbing its legs and face, trying to hold it back. I grabbed Connor and flung him to the side. With him out of the way, I turned back to the wendigo.

It was down on all fours, its fur standing on edge, and radiating anger and hate. Magdalena was nowhere to be seen, but I knew she was alive. Eleanor had a grip on the creature's left arm and Elizabeth had the right. The twins were crawling up the creatures back, using its fur as handholds and its knobby, skeleton-like surface as footholds.

The owl was stirring in my chest, wanting out, but I kept it in. I was too tired to let it out. If I did, I had no idea what would happen. The owl and I were connected. If it died, I died, and if it was as tired as me, it didn't stand a chance against the wendigo.

As I desperately thought about how to deal with this creature, Jonathan reached its head and grabbed one of its horns. The wendigo roared and shook itself with all its might. The twins went flying. Still wobbling after its shake, the wendigo lifted its left arm. Elizabeth dangled off of it for a second before it swung, shaking her off like a drop of water. She hadn't even hit the ground before the creature lifted its other arm and slammed it against the wall, Eleanor disappearing through it and letting go.

Pictures rattled and fell to the floor, cracking and breaking.

The wendigo turned back to me, and I felt all those dark feelings humming through me. As if they were my own, they made me feel hungry and full at the same time, sick to my stomach.

My already weak legs gave way and I tumbled to the ground, gripping my stomach to try and keep what little I'd eaten that day down.

From beside me, Connor murmured something, standing still and stiff, staring at the wendigo.

It heard him and turned toward the sound, and I somehow knew that it had found what it was looking for.

I whimpered and let my owl loose. It pushed from my chest and flew straight at the wendigo. The monster flicked one claw, hitting my owl, my soul, right out of the air. I screamed as the owl hit the window, feeling my ribs break and my arms bend in unnatural ways.

Something hit the wendigo and exploded in a small ball of blue fire. The wendigo roared and reared up in pain. It turned, looking at Sara standing at the foot of the stairs, a wooden box in her hands and her eyes glowing yellow. Jake was standing on the stairs just behind her, one hand on her shoulder, panting.

"I can't miss," she said with a crooked smile and threw another crystal. It hit the wendigo and exploded. The creature roared again.

Sara threw her third crystal. I didn't see what happened next, but somehow the wendigo had the crystal in its claws. It turned with the momentum of the stone, spinning in place, and let it go as it came around. Sara and Jake jumped out of the way as the crystal hit the stairs just below where they stood, exploding, scalding the carpet and burning the wood of the steps.

Connor, somehow able to move despite the terror I felt rolling off him in waves, ran into the living room. He hit the sofa and tumbled over its back, disappearing. With Sara out of the way, the wendigo lurched after him.

I couldn't do anything as it flung its hand down behind the sofa, as I heard Connor scream in fear, and the wendigo lifted him up with one clawed hand, its claws digging into the man's suit and drawing blood.

I couldn't move as the wendigo brought its skull close to Connor's forehead, as they shared a breath – if the wendigo did breathe – and as something passed between them. The wendigo started dissolving into a fine mist and slipped between my father's lips. As it did, Connor slipped to the ground, standing still, staring emptily at the creature. The last thing to disappear into him was the darkness where the eyes should have been. I saw that same darkness move in my father's once bright blue with green spots eyes as they settled on me, and his once-beloved face smirked in a way that made me cold to my very core.

He, it, took a step toward me but stopped as I felt someone move up beside me. I saw Sara's boots. The wendigo used Connor's eyes to look her up and down, resting at something for a second, then sneered and turned. Moving fast but jarringly, as if unused to the body, he sprang from the living room and into the hallway.

Sara disappeared from my side and I was left alone with my pain. Blood was dripping from my lips and I could hardly breathe.

30

"He's gone," someone said beside me. "What happened?"

"She's bleeding."

"From where? It didn't touch her!"

"Look."

Someone touched my face and tried to lift it, but the movement shot icy fire through my neck, shoulders, back, and ribcage, and I coughed blood as I tried to scream in pain, but it came out as a whimper.

I heard the voices talking fast and low before someone said something about an owl and I stopped breathing for a moment. This made the voices go silent again before speaking even faster. I heard boots running against hardwood floors, making the world under me jump up and down and moving my broken bones.

Someone was touching me, whispering to me. I think I blacked out. Forcing my eyes open, I saw Sara's blue, worried eyes. There were tears in them.

"I'm sorry, I'm so sorry," she said.

I was about to ask why she was sorry, but she disappeared from view and I couldn't bring my eyes to follow her. They were about to close again as someone grabbed one of my shoulders and lifted me from the floor. The pain was so sharp that I was able to scream this time.

Warm, strong hands grabbed my wrists from either side, sitting me up to rest my back against their chest. Jake. I felt his heartbeat. Every time he breathed it hurt me. I couldn't stop the scream that was singing from my lungs. Couldn't stop the blood that was dribbling from my lips and onto my barely moving chest. Whispering in my ear that he was sorry, so sorry, he forced my arms to the side and my chest out. I heard the bones inside me clatter against each other, felt them tear through flesh and muscle.

The scream died as I ran out of air, but my lips were still parted: ready if I was ever able to make a sound again.

Sara came into my field of vision, cradling something white against her chest. She knelt and held the white forward. A part of me recognized it as my owl, but it was as broken as me. Blood spotted its usually white feathers. Drops of water had fallen beside the blood and was smearing it, making some of the spots more pink than red. Tears, I realized. Someone had cried on my owl. It was such a silly thought in-between all the pain.

Leaning forward, Sara placed the owl against my chest. I felt the fluttering heartbeat in that small frame, and my own broken shell reached out to it.

As we'd done so many times already, the owl and I merged. Its broken wings became whole as they borrowed my arms health. My broken ribs fell into position as it took its place in my chest, filling the cavity there. For the first time in what felt like forever, I could draw a full breath.

I began to sob and pulled at my hands. Jake let them go and I curled around myself, crying for the hurt inside my body. My ribs were back in place but they were still broken. The hole in my lung was filled by the owl's feathers and it still hurt to breathe too deeply but I couldn't help the sobs. One thing was my broken body. It hurt. But it was nothing compared to my heart.

Aunt Ellie had said it was broken and she was breaking it even more when forcing me to send her away. Now, whatever had held it together was gone. The look in Connor's eyes when he took that step forward... I knew he, it, meant to kill me. I could feel its intentions, running through the air like lightning. Then he would kill Sara, and Mrs. Hearth and Abigail, and Jake, and everyone in this neighborhood, and the world if it could.

The body may have been that of Connor Key, but the soul was that of the wendigo. My father was gone.

31

I must have cried myself to sleep while lying on the hardwood floor in the sunroom of the Hearth-family home, for the next thing I remember was someone carrying me past the dining room. All the way up the stairs, I could hear the Hearth-women yelling at each other.

Jake, for that was the only one I didn't hear cursing down-stairs, carried me into Sara's room and lay me carefully down on the bed. My breath hitched in pain as he slipped his arms from under me.

"Shhh, rest."

I lay on that bed and let him pull off my clothes as careful as he could until I was left in a t-shirt and jeans. Just as carefully, he pulled the duvet out from under me and wrapped me in it. By the time he stood, I was slipping back into sleep.

The human was tossing and turning its head. Their face was pale and turned to the ceiling, as it always was when I was riding them. Weak light filtered through the thin curtains, glistening on the human's open eyes. It was gasping for air as I pressed down on its chest, which was already broken beneath my weight. Someone had been here before and sowed the seed for my nightmares. I didn't mind. It made it easier for me to feed.

Usually, I couldn't reach this one, but tonight its guardians were busy elsewhere. Their grief hung in the air like gravy to the taste of this one's fear, and a little anger as well, which was why they weren't in the room with it.

My black hair hung in its face and slipped into its mouth, down its throat. The human started coughing and whimpering in pain at every move. The eyes were looking right at me, seeing me as humans should not be able to, but it endeared me. Its nightmares endeared me.

The door opened and spilled electric light on my back. It slipped through me and onto the human. I pulled back. Pulled my hair out of their mouth and my claws from their throat. Lifted myself into the shadows so they could breathe freely onc...

My body shuddered, finally able to move. I'd dreamt I was looking down at myself, and when I woke, I was lying there, not able to move and hardly able to breathe, as I looked up at a figure straddling my chest. It looked like a tall, skinny woman, more grey than white, with black pools for eyes and black hair falling like snakes onto my face, into my mouth.

"Awake?" Sara asked and entered the room, letting the door rest against the jamb but not closing it properly.

I mumbled in the affirmative and tried to sit up, but groaned at the sudden pain and stayed down instead. Sara hurried to the bed and sank onto it, resting a hand on my shoulder. It hurt. Not like a broken bone, but more like a fresh bruise. When she was sure I was going to stay, she curled up next to me, resting her forehead against my arm.

"What happened?" I asked after a while. "Where's Jake?"

"He's sleeping in Emma's room," Sara answered, her voice muffled in the duvet.

She was shivering slightly, and I lifted the edge of the duvet with my hand. It hurt moving, so I was glad when she took the weight and crawled under it to join me. I let her use the rustling of fabric as an excuse not to answer my first question, but when the only sound in the room was our breathing, I nudged her.

"The wendigo came here. It knocked mom against the wall and hurt you and Jake. It took your dad."

The darkness behind my eyelids was not much blacker than that of the room, but it felt heavier. "Why were you arguing?"

She sighed. "You heard that?"

"Barely. I thought maybe it was a nightmare?"

"No, it wasn't. Mom... she blames you." I wasn't surprised by her words, but they still stung. "Grams says she's afraid of you 'cause she doesn't understand, but that's bullshit and we both know it. Mom got weird the moment she knew you saw spirits. She thinks you called the wendigo here. That you tore open the Veil on purpose to draw as many spirit creatures to our world as you could."

"Why would I do that?"

She shrugged. "She said something 'bout harvesting their energy. By then, I wasn't listening..."

"...You were yelling," I finished, remembering how she'd explained many of her fights with her mom earlier.

Sara chuckled darkly. "Yeah, pretty much."

We lay in silence for a moment, listening to the wind whisper past the walls outside and the house creaking and moaning to itself. The sound of the rocker became clear after a while, and I could hear faint voices creeping up through the floor.

"The rocker's been moving since just after the wendigo left," Sara finally said, her tone giving away that she was trying to lighten the mood and avoid the question that hung between us.

"Probably Eleanor," I answered in the same type of voice. "She's really old school that way, and I think it reminds her of when she was alive." Sara made a neutral sound and burrowed deeper into the duvet, as if cold. Finally, I had to ask: "Do you agree with Abigail?"

"'bout what?"

"You know about what."

A moment that felt like forever passed. "No. I think you may be connected to the wendigo and other spirit creatures somehow for being a necromancer and all, but I don't think you called 'em here on purpose, or that you want to use your new powers for evil. I think you're still the girl I love."

I opened my eyes and looked at the ceiling, joy and sorrow waring inside me. "So now what?"

Sara shrugged again, trying to hide a yawn. "Mom left. She don't wanna sleep in the same house as you."

"Thanks."

"Sorry, but I won't lie. Grams is calling the coven. We pretty much know there's an opening in the Veil now. Some way for the wendigo and other big spirits to get through. We might need your help with that."

"And Connor?"

"Dunno. We need to get the wendigo out of him somehow. Jake's gonna look closer at it tomorrow, but he needs sleep."

"You do too."

She yawned again. "Nah, sleep's for the weak." I didn't answer, but I'm pretty sure she could picture the look I would have given her. "We need to figure out how to deal with your ghosts. The house's starting to feel crowded."

"Jake didn't know anything?"

"Not much, but some. Could you do what you did with the

other ghost again? When you borrowed my luck just before the wendigo attacked?"

I shook my head. "I used necromancy. None of us really know how it works. According to you, it's supposed to be bad. What if I sent aunt Ellie to Hell or something like that? What if I damned her?" Voicing my worries made the small knot in my stomach grow even bigger and stronger. It was making it hard to think about anything else. "What if I only made things worse?"

Sara carefully lay a hand on my chest, and it was heavy but welcome. A new voice came sneaking through the floor, but Sara talked over it. "Don't think like that, ok? I don't think you could send someone to Hell unless you specifically asked for it, and as I said, you ain't evil. I'm sure your aunt is right where she's supposed to be."

"But how can we know?"

"There are ways to talk to those that've moved on. If Jake doesn't come up with anything, we can try summoning her." I nodded, distracted by the new voices downstairs. Were those men? "You there?" Sara asked when I didn't answer.

"Yes, I just... Do you hear that?"

We listened for a moment. It sounded like a party down there with all those voices, and some of them were rising in volume, like someone arguing.

"No, I don't hear nothing," Sara finally answered.

A chill ran down my back, banishing my worry for aunt Ellie for a moment. "Help me up."

"What? No, you need rest."

"Please. There's something going on, and I'm afraid to think what it might mean."

"What do you think it means?"

"I'll tell you later, just help me up."

Grumbling about this being a bad idea, she crawled out from the warmth of the duvet and helped me up. The cold of the room blended with the chill of fear and it felt like my hands were vibrating with it, but they were steady as I gripped Sara's arms and let her help me up. It hurt and I made a face against her shoulder before I pushed up as straight as I could and wobbled toward the door.

"Maybe we should've taken you to the hospital," Sara mumbled behind me.

I opened the door and answered in a low whisper so as not to wake Jake or warn those downstairs, even as the floor moaned beneath me. "And told them what? That my soul took a beating and now I carry the damage of it?"

"Is that what happened?"

I didn't answer, but rested a finger over my lips and began the descent of the stairs.

There were just a few voices speaking now, sounding like four people trying to talk over each other, and they all sounded male.

At the landing between the ground and first floor, the air started to change. It wasn't exactly a chill, more like a cold mist. Sara took my hand and glanced around, as if looking for the open window, even if we both knew there were none nearby.

The voices were coming from the sunroom, where the sound of the chair rocking back and forth lay like a bass underneath their arguing. I straightened my back and opened the door someone had closed while I slept.

A sudden silence fell as everyone in the room turned to look at me.

Eleanor sat in the rocking chair, Magdalena in her lap much like when aunt Ellie was dying. The three siblings were sitting on the divan where my aunt had drawn her last ghostly breaths not half a night ago. Around them, standing or sitting at every chair, some even sitting on the floor and one sitting on top of the commode beside the door, were ghosts. There were men, women, and children, and they were dressed in everything from hooped skirts and high stockings to miniskirts and beanies.

"Ah, just the witch we wanted to see," said an elderly man in a suit and a full beard.

"She is not a witch," Johana said, rolling her eyes like she'd said it a million times before.

"Then how can she see us?"

"She is a shaman, duh."

The man turned to her, looking like he was going to give her a telling-to, and by the expresions of the people around them, it wouldn't be the first.

"She's right," I said, entering the room and closing the door behind Sara and me so as not to wake the other living people in the house. "I'm a shaman. She's a witch," I pointed to Sara, who waved gingerly at what for her looked like an empty room. "What can I do for all of you?"

"Well, first of all, I would like to know why I suddenly needed to come here," the man began, looking gruff and making me shudder a little with the thought of my first use of necromancy. "Secondly, this woman tells me you can help us move on," he motioned to Eleanor. "Is that true?"

I glanced at my fright of ghosts, seeing their tired but steady gazes. Drawing a deep breath, I returned my attention to the man. "In theory, I should be able to do that. I still don't know how, but that is supposed to be what I do, so I will be able to do it sooner or later."

"When?" Asked a young woman by the garden doors. She

wore an old, grey wool dress. Her face and bonnet were dirty, and she kept wringing a shawl between her too skinny hands. She reminded me of Sanderson, and I swallowed the pang of pain and sorrow.

"Hopefully, very soon," I answered. "We are going to do everything we can to make it happen as fast as we can."

At that, the ghosts started talking over each other again. Some seemed to beg me for favors. Some said they wouldn't go. Some said they had to go now, that there were people waiting for them. Others asked why they needed my help to move on in the first place, or what I got out of it.

I let their words move over and past me like water, recognizing the confusion of feelings on their faces and letting them calm themselves down. I was too tired to deal with them.

Sara squeezed my hand and leaned as close to my ear as she could get. "The room's full of ghosts?" she whispered. I nodded. "And they all want your help?" Another nod. "Sucks." A third nod. "What're you gonna do 'bout it?"

I sighed and turned to leave. The clamor grew louder.

"I need to sleep," I said as I reached for the door handle. "I'll deal with you tomorrow when I know what to do."

Before they could ask any questions, I pulled Sara out of the sunroom and closed the door between me and the ghosts.

To be continued...

Acknowledgment

I guess there's a lot of people I can thank for this book in some way or another.

I know I need to thank my partner. I owe them everything. Both for my falling in love with writing, but also for them standing by my side through something no couple at our age should have to live through.

Thank you for staying with me, you're my hero, and I hope you know it.

I also need to thank my beta readers. Evelyn, Anniken, Kristina, and Zack. Your feedback was invaluable, and I wouldn't have had the guts to publish if not for your help. Thank you so, so much! And thank you to Solstice for helping me with the French part! It would have been a mess of Google Translate, if not for you.

The excellent artists at the CoverCollective.com, who created my cover, also need thanks.

Lastly, I need to comment on the wendigo.
Wendigos are originally a mythological man-eating creature or evil spirit from the folklore of the First Nations Algonquian tribes from Canada. The wendigo you read about in this book, is adopted and changed to fit my story, so do not take my wendigo as fact.

About the Author

Kima Blaze lives in along the fjords of Norway, with her partner and lover, and their dog.

Kima came late to the writing game, discovering it in her early twenties when sickness took hold of her life. Her partner, who had been writing their entire life, suggested Kima write down her frustration. She hasn't stopped writing since.

CURSE OF A NAME is her first published work.

THE CURSE OF SIGHT is her second.

You can connect with me on:

🐦 https://twitter.com/KimaBlaze

🔗 https://www.patreon.com/kimablaze

Subscribe to my newsletter:

✉ https://landing.mailerlite.com/webforms/landing/u6f9x4

Also by Kima Blaze

A RIFT IN THE VEIL-series
Curse of a Name

Expected publications in 2020:
  A RIFT IN THE VEIL, book 3: A Cursed Legacy

CURSE OF A NAME

After returning to her childhood home to care for her Alzheimers sick mother, Elizabeth ''Lizzie'' Key starts having nightmares of women dying through history. All of them with her name. While trying to help her violent mother and at the same time keep her own sanity, Lizzie can't be sure if her dreams and her mother's ramblings are in truth a warning, or if she herself is getting sick.

But she can't shake the feeling that many of her family's ghosts are real, and some of them are more bloodthirsty than others